ANNE MC
DEATH OF A WED

C000173593

ANNE Morice, *née* Felicity Shaw, was born in Kent in 1916.

Her mother Muriel Rose was the natural daughter of Rebecca Gould and Charles Morice. Muriel Rose married a Kentish doctor, and they had a daughter, Elizabeth. Muriel Rose's three later daughters—Angela, Felicity and Yvonne—were fathered by playwright Frederick Lonsdale.

Felicity's older sister Angela became an actress, married actor and theatrical agent Robin Fox, and produced England's Fox acting dynasty, including her sons Edward and James and grandchildren Laurence, Jack, Emilia and Freddie.

Felicity went to work in the office of the GPO Film Unit. There Felicity met and married documentarian Alexander Shaw. They had three children and lived in various countries.

Felicity wrote two well-received novels in the 1950's, but did not publish again until successfully launching her Tessa Crichton mystery series in 1970, buying a house in Hambleden, near Henley-on-Thames, on the proceeds. Her last novel was published a year after her death at the age of seventy-three on May 18th, 1989.

BY ANNE MORICE

and available from Dean Street Press

ANNE MORICE

DEATH OF A WEDDING GUEST

With an introduction and afterword by
Curtis Evans

DEAN STREET PRESS

Published by Dean Street Press 2021

Copyright © 1976 Anne Morice

Introduction & Afterword © 2021 Curtis Evans

First published in 1976 by Macmillan

Cover by DSP

The publisher thanks Mike Morris for providing essential material to this publication

ISBN 978 1 914150 07 4

www.deanstreetpress.co.uk

INTRODUCTION

BY 1970 the Golden Age of detective fiction, which had dawned in splendor a half-century earlier in 1920, seemingly had sunk into shadow like the sun at eventide. There were still a few old bodies from those early, glittering days who practiced the fine art of finely clued murder, to be sure, but in most cases the hands of those murderously talented individuals were growing increasingly infirm. Queen of Crime Agatha Christie, now eighty years old, retained her bestselling status around the world, but surely no one could have deluded herself into thinking that the novel *Passenger to Frankfurt*, the author's 1970 "Christie for Christmas" (which publishers for want of a better word dubbed "an Extravaganza") was prime Christie—or, indeed, anything remotely close to it. Similarly, two other old crime masters, Americans John Dickson Carr and Ellery Queen (comparative striplings in their sixties), both published detective novels that year, but both books were notably weak efforts on their parts. Agatha Christie's American counterpart in terms of work productivity and worldwide sales, Erle Stanley Gardner, creator of Perry Mason, published nothing at all that year, having passed away in March at the age of eighty. Admittedly such old-timers as Rex Stout, Ngaio Marsh, Michael Innes and Gladys Mitchell were still playing the game with some of their old élan, but in truth their glory days had fallen behind them as well. Others, like Margery Allingham and John Street, had died within the last few years or, like Anthony Gilbert, Nicholas Blake, Leo Bruce and Christopher Bush, soon would expire or become debilitated. Decidedly in 1970—a year which saw the trials of the Manson family and the Chicago Seven, assorted bombings, kidnappings and plane hijackings by such terroristic entities as the Weathermen, the Red Army, the PLO and the FLQ, the American invasion of Cambodia and the Kent State shootings and the drug overdose deaths of Jimi Hendrix and Janis Joplin—leisure readers now more than ever stood in need of the intelligent escapism which classic crime fiction provided. Yet the old order in crime fiction, like that in world politics and society, seemed irrevocably to be washing away in a bloody tide of violent anarchy and all round uncouthness.

Or was it? Old values have a way of persisting. Even as the generation which produced the glorious detective fiction of the Golden Age finally began exiting the crime scene, a new generation of younger puzzle adepts had arisen, not to take the esteemed places of their elders, but to contribute their own worthy efforts to the rarefied field of fair play murder. Among these writers were P.D. James, Ruth Rendell, Emma Lathen, Patricia Moyes, H.R.F. Keating, Catherine Aird, Joyce Porter, Margaret Yorke, Elizabeth Lemarchand, Reginald Hill, Peter Lovesey and the author whom you are perusing now, Anne Morice (1916-1989). Morice, who like Yorke, Lovesey and Hill debuted as a mystery writer in 1970, was lavishly welcomed by critics in the United Kingdom (she was not published in the United States until 1974) upon the publication of her first mystery, *Death in the Grand Manor*, which suggestively and anachronistically was subtitled not an "extravaganza," but a novel of detection. Fittingly the book was lauded by no less than seemingly permanently retired Golden Age stalwarts Edmund Crispin and Francis Iles (aka Anthony Berkeley Cox). Crispin deemed Morice's debut puzzler "a charming whodunit . . . full of unforced buoyance" and prescribed it as a "remedy for existentialist gloom," while Iles, who would pass away at the age of seventy-seven less than six months after penning his review, found the novel a "most attractive lightweight," adding enthusiastically: "[E]ntertainingly written, it provides a modern version of the classical type of detective story. I was much taken with the cheerful young narrator . . . and I think most readers will feel the same way. Warmly recommended." Similarly, Maurice Richardson, who, although not a crime writer, had reviewed crime fiction for decades at the *London Observer*, lavished praise upon Morice's maiden mystery: "Entrancingly fresh and lively whodunit. . . . Excellent dialogue. . . . Much superior to the average effort to lighten the detective story."

With such a critical sendoff, it is no surprise that Anne Morice's crime fiction took flight on the wings of its bracing mirth. Over the next two decades twenty-five Anne Morice mysteries were published (the last of them posthumously), at the rate of one or two year. Twenty-three of these concerned the investigations of Tessa Crichton, a charming young actress who always manages to cross paths with murder, while two, written at the end of her career, detail cases of Detective Superintendent "Tubby" Wiseman. In 1976 Morice along with Margaret Yorke was chosen to become a member of Britain's prestigious Detection Club, preceding Ruth Rendell by a year, while in the 1980s her books were included in Bantam's superlative paperback "Murder

Most British" series, which included luminaries from both present and past like Rendell, Yorke, Margery Allingham, Patricia Wentworth, Christianna Brand, Elizabeth Ferrars, Catherine Aird, Margaret Erskine, Marian Babson, Dorothy Simpson, June Thomson and last, but most certainly not least, the Queen of Crime herself, Agatha Christie. In 1974, when Morice's fifth Tessa Crichton detective novel, *Death of a Dutiful Daughter*, was picked up in the United States, the author's work again was received with acclaim, with reviewers emphasizing the author's cozy traditionalism (though the term "cozy" had not then come into common use in reference to traditional English and American mysteries). In his notice of Morice's *Death of a Wedding Guest* (1976), "Newgate Callendar" (aka classical music critic Harold C. Schoenberg), Seventies crime fiction reviewer for the *New York Times Book Review*, observed that "Morice is a traditionalist, and she has no surprises [in terms of subject matter] in her latest book. What she does have, as always, is a bright and amusing style . . . [and] a general air of sophisticated writing." Perhaps a couple of reviews from Middle America—where intense Anglophilia, the dogmatic pronouncements of Raymond Chandler and Edmund Wilson notwithstanding, still ran rampant among mystery readers—best indicate the cozy criminal appeal of Anne Morice:

> Anne Morice . . . acquired me as a fan when I read her "Death and the Dutiful Daughter." In this new novel, she did not disappoint me. The same appealing female detective, Tessa Crichton, solves the mysteries on her own, which is surpris-

ing in view of the fact that Tessa is actually not a detective, but a film actress. Tessa just seems to be at places where a murder occurs, and at the most unlikely places at that . . . this time at a garden fete on the estate of a millionaire tycoon. . . . The plot is well constructed; I must confess that I, like the police, had my suspect all picked out too. I was "dead" wrong (if you will excuse the expression) because my suspect was also murdered before not too many pages turned. . . . This is not a blood-curdling, chilling mystery; it is amusing and light, but Miss Morice writes in a polished and intelligent manner, providing pleasure and entertainment. (Rose Levine Isaacson, review of *Death of a Heavenly Twin, Jackson Mississippi Clarion-Ledger*, 18 August 1974)

I like English mysteries because the victims are always rotten people who deserve to die. Anne Morice, like Ngaio Marsh et al., writes tongue in cheek but with great care. It is always a joy to read English at its glorious best. (Sally Edwards, "Ever-So British, This Tale," review of *Killing with Kindness, Charlotte North Carolina Observer*, 10 April 1975)

While it is true that Anne Morice's mysteries most frequently take place at country villages and estates, surely the quintessence of modern cozy mystery settings, there is a pleasing tartness to Tessa's narration and the brittle, epigrammatic dialogue which reminds me of the Golden Age Crime Queens (particularly Ngaio Marsh) and, to part from mystery for a moment, English playwright Noel Coward. Morice's books may be cozy but they most certainly are not cloying, nor are the sentiments which the characters express invariably "traditional." The author avoids any traces of soppiness or sentimentality and has a knack for clever turns of phrase which is characteristic of the bright young things of the Twenties and Thirties, the decades of her own youth. "Sackcloth and ashes would have been overdressing for the mood I had sunk into by then," Tessa reflects at one point in the novel *Death in the Grand Manor.* Never fear, however: nothing, not even the odd murder or two, keeps Tessa down in the dumps for long; and invariably she finds herself back on the trail of murder most foul, to the consternation of her handsome, debonair husband, Inspector Robin Price of Scotland Yard (whom she meets in the first novel in the series and has married by the second), and the exasperation of her amusingly eccentric and indolent playwright cousin, Toby Crichton, both of whom feature in almost all of the Tessa Crichton novels. Murder may not lastingly mar Tessa's equanimity, but she certainly takes her detection seriously.

Three decades now having passed since Anne Morice's crime novels were in print, fans of British mystery in both its classic and cozy forms should derive much pleasure in discovering (or rediscovering) her work in these new Dean Street Press editions and thereby passing time once again in that pleasant fictional English world where death affords us not emotional disturbance and distress but enjoyable and intelligent diversion.

Curtis Evans

PART ONE

CHAPTER ONE

The Times, 24th April.

Mr J. Roxburgh and
Miss E.S.R. Crichton.

The marriage has been arranged and will take place shortly between Jeremy, elder son of Mr and Mrs Arnold Roxburgh of 149, Chester Square, S.W.1, and Long Barn House, near Sunningdale, Berkshire, and Ellen Sarah Rachel, only daughter of Mr Toby Crichton of Roakes Common, Oxfordshire, and of Mrs Irene Lewis of 1818B Princess Alexandra Drive, Winnipeg.

'Do we know this J. Roxburgh?' I enquired of my cousin Toby, having telephoned him in the desperation born of three futile attempts to obtain the information from the horse's mouth.

'We presume Ellen does, so why not ask her?'

'I tried that, naturally, but there's no reply from her flat. I suppose she's sleeping it off.'

'Or else that witch she lives with has decided that it is not a propitious day for answering the telephone. As it happens, though, I doubt if Ellen could tell you much more than I can. She has only known him for a couple of weeks. I think it must be what they call the rebound.'

'From Desmond?'

'That's the one.'

'In that case, it could be a bound in the right direction. I never had much time for Desmond. He's a grossly over-rated actor, whatever the critics may say, and invariably stoned from noon till dusk, the only time I ever had to work with him. At least this Jeremy sounds a bit more on the solid side. All those posh addresses do inspire a certain confidence. Nothing in Scotland, though.'

'Is that your criterion in solidity or poshness?'

'Neither, but Roxburgh has north-of-the-border connotations.'

'My dear Tessa, a lot of people are called Parsons, but it doesn't follow that they're all clergymen. I understand this lot started life as Rosenbergs, or something of that kind. Don't you find that strange? I'm sure if my name had been Roxburgh I should have lost no time in changing it to Rosenberg, but they tell me it takes all sorts.'

'You surely don't mean that Roxburgh, Toby?'

'Don't I?'

'Not the one who keeps running up all those mighty hotels and office blocks?'

'Just so. Most of them collapse just before the official opening, but unfortunately not all.'

'But they must be absolutely rolling?'

'Well, as to that, it doesn't do to judge by posh addresses. For all we know, the core may be rotten and he'll come crashing down some day just as surely as one of his own concrete monstrosities.'

'We must hope not, for Ellen's sake.'

'It would certainly provide a testing time for her, if she is marrying for money. Do you suppose that could be the springboard for this rebound?'

'Unlikely, I should have thought.'

'And you should know. You're her second cousin, after all, and much more her generation than I can ever be. On the other hand, we shouldn't overlook the fact that her mother was money mad.'

'Oh yes, Irene; I saw she'd been included in the announcement. Will she be coming over for the wedding?'

'Not if I can prevent it.'

'And you think you can?'

'The mood is one of cautious optimism. Ellen asked if I thought we should cable her and I advised her to leave all those boring details to me. With any luck, that'll be the last we'll hear of it. If the worst comes to the worst, we must get Ellen's friend, Jezebel, to send Irene a diagram showing all the evil omens fighting it out over mid-Atlantic during the crucial week. That should scare her off.'

CHAPTER TWO

'DO HAVE a squashed fly!' Jezebel said, lazily proffering the plate of biscuits, 'it looks as though there are one or two underneath which haven't been mauled by Caspar.'

'No thanks,' I said, appearances having belied her claim. Jezebel who, with her husband and son, shared a flat with Ellen in Beauchamp Place, was a dedicated zodiac interpreter and priestess. She contributed a monthly page to a popular magazine and, although meticulous and painstaking in her work, was inclined to be slapdash in mundane affairs, a characteristic which was reflected in her manner and appearance. She had an overblown look about her, emphasised by the voluminous garments in which she habitually trailed about. This was in sharp contrast to Ellen who, at the age of nineteen, had the vital statistics of a pencil, although at that moment making a hearty meal of bread and butter and honey.

Jezebel's husband was called Bert and was part owner of a snooty and expensive restaurant in Kensington known as Chey Bert. The joke here was that the other half of the partnership was a man called Cheyne, as some of the uninitiated clientèle were chastened to discover when they pointed to the apparent misspelling.

Caspar, the only child of this union, was a pale, noble-browed infant of three years old, although possessing an I.Q., so I was reliably informed, of one twice his age. Observing him now, as he tottered round the room, stuffing handfuls of food into his face, idly smearing his sticky fingers along the furniture, and watching with profound absorption as the milk from his tilted mug dribbled in a thin line over the carpet, it occurred to me that here, rather than in money madness, might lie the root of Ellen's decision to change her life-style. It was two years since she had become co-tenant of this large, comfortable and untidy flat and no one could fail to see that it had grown progressively smaller, more untidy and less comfortable with every subsequent stage of Caspar's development.

This reflection reminded me of the purpose of my visit and simultaneously, with a flash of the E.S.P. which Jezebel's presence so often invoked, Ellen said:

'I suppose you wouldn't consider being a matron of honour?'

'No, thanks awfully. It always sounds a bit dowdy, and also rather like a cake.'

She sighed and poured herself another cup of tea:

'I was afraid of that. The trouble is that you can't be a bridesmaid, now you're married to Robin, and I seem to be rather short on female relatives. Jeremy has a whole string of cousins and nieces, all set to prance up the aisle, and it would have been nice to have had just one from our side.'

'I've offered her Caspar as a page,' Jezebel explained, 'but she doesn't want to know.'

'Can you blame me?' Ellen asked. 'The last thing I need is Caspar crouching at my heels, chewing up the lace train. If he's going to be in church at all I want him handcuffed.'

'So you're having the full regalia, are you? Bridesmaids, organs, tiaras and all? Which church, by the way?'

'Oh, Roakes, naturally. Where else? I mean, it's the done thing, isn't it, for these galas to take place on the bride's home ground?'

'I was only faintly startled because Toby never mentioned it. It's the sort of prospect which in the ordinary way would have him arranging the pillow in the gas oven.'

Evidently bored by this turn in the conversation, Jez heaved herself up from the table, gathered Caspar on to her left hip and proceeded to make a languorous exit, saying it was time to put him to bed. Since the time was four-fifteen, I awarded her low marks for failing to invent a slightly more subtle excuse while she was about it, but I should have known better. She was at once too indolent and too self-assured to bother with tactful gestures and had meant precisely what she said.

'He was up half the night with his jigsaw,' she explained before closing the door.

Ellen, who had been frowning into her teacup during this break in the flow, now said:

'To be absolutely frank with you, Tessa, Toby doesn't know himself yet, so be a friend and don't say a word to him. I must find the right moment to break it gently. We're having a marquee in the garden too, so it's not going to be easy.'

'Why do it, then, since you know it's bound to annoy him?'

'Oh well, you see, the Roxburghs are great on the conventions. They like everything to be done according to tradition. Jeremy says it's because they haven't many of their own that they're so keen to get stuck into other people's.'

'And you mean to indulge them, rather than Toby?'

'Not really, but it won't kill him to sacrifice one day in his life and since it means so much to them . . . they've been fantastically generous to us, you know; me and Jeremy, I mean. Did I tell you they'd bought this house for us in Little Venice and are having it all redecorated and everything? It's going to be smashing if it's ever finished. And they brought me the most fabulous gold bracelet from Geneva the other day. Positively strewing bribes in our path.'

'No wonder you feel kindly towards them! Not every young man's parents are so eager to gain a daughter.'

'I shan't let it go to my head, though, because it's not me as an individual that they're wooing. It's simply that they're so, so grateful to me for being young, single and passably respectable, compared to some.'

'Compared to some what?'

'Well, you see, Jeremy was shacked up for about two years with a female called Imogen. She's Scandinavian or something. Not that they'd have minded that, I suppose, but she's at least thirty-five, and divorced and she's got two children who go to boarding schools, and his poor old Mum and Dad were shaking all over at the thought that he might walk in one afternoon and say he'd married her.'

'Did he want to?'

'To begin with I think he did, yes, but she wasn't properly divorced then and by the time the legal thing was settled he'd begun to cool off. She'd become so frightfully jealous and possessive, kept making the most ghastly scenes if he was five minutes late getting home from work; and having the children there for the holidays was rather a drag too. Anyway, about three months ago they had the most blinding row and he walked out. She's been hounding him ever since and ringing up day and night in floods of tears, but it only turns him off more than ever. He says he can see now how deeply neurotic she is and he's thankful to have escaped. Anyway, it was soon after they split up that I met him.'

'And how was that?'

'Was what?'

'How did you meet him?'

'Oh, through Desmond, oddly enough. They'd been at Harrow together, before Desmond got chucked out for being drunk and disorderly in chapel. It was when Desmond was playing at the Comedy that I first met Jeremy. He was at a loose end because being with Imogen had meant cutting himself off from all his old mates, so he dropped in to see the play one evening and came round afterwards. I happened to be in Desmond's dressing room, so we all went out and had supper together and that's how it started.'

'So it was Jeremy's rebound, not yours? You were still seeing Desmond in those days? I am sorry to ask all these questions, but I feel that someone ought to and I can't think who else it could be.'

'Poor old Tess!' Ellen said, regarding me with fond compassion. 'But I honestly don't mind at all. I'm grateful to you for taking an interest, and the answer is yes. The weird thing is that I didn't particularly take to Jeremy at first, but he was very kind and sweet and I felt sorry for him. He took me out to dinner once or twice and told me some more about the sad story of him and Imogen and so on, and then we'd both go and see Desmond after the show. He just sort of edged his way in, if you know what I mean?'

'Yes I do, only too well.'

'Well, things went on like that for a few weeks, until the play had to close because they were doing such rotten business and that set Desmond off on the most frightful bout of depression, so that he was blind drunk for days; but instead of getting all worked up and terrified of his being arrested or run over, I said to myself: What the hell? *Che sarà sarà* was what I said.'

'And floated out to dinner with Jeremy?'

'More or less. It had become the natural thing to do. As I've told you, he's fantastically kind and I had a sad story of my own to tell by then. It made a kind of bond.'

'Two little rebounders, weeping into the coq au vin?'

'Okay, laugh as much as you like, Tess, but that wasn't all we had in common. And I'll tell you something else to cheer you up. I brought him round here to meet Jez one evening and she was wildly impressed. She said he was packed to the lid with all the right auras and vibrations and could obviously never put a foot wrong. So then she worked out his horoscope. It was a really deep one, starting with the exact minute of his birth and the actual street in London and so on, in order to get everything right in relation to the sun. It was lucky his mother is so doting because she'd recorded every cloying detail in a great fat album called "Baby Days" or something revolting. Anyway, it took Jez three solid days to work on it and by about half way through she was practically dancing with excitement. It came out that our magnetic fields were simply perfect for each other. In fact, if any two people in the world ought to belong together it's Jeremy and me, so what do you say to that?'

'Well, naturally, I wouldn't attempt to argue with that kind of evidence,' I replied with a sigh. 'But it seems to me that I've now heard about fourteen more or less barmy reasons for your marrying Jeremy, so couldn't you give me one really convincing one?'

'Yes, of course I can, because we're both madly in love. How dotty of me not to mention that before, but honestly, Tess, I just took it for granted that you'd know.'

Ellen had opened her enormous grey-green eyes as wide as they would go while saying this, and I have to confess that I had no idea whether to believe her or not.

CHAPTER THREE

MORE than a week went by before I had a chance to form my own opinion of Jeremy Roxburgh and on balance it was unfavourable, although his shortcomings were the reverse of everything I had expected.

I had invited him and Ellen to dine with us at Beacon Square and at the very last minute Scotland Yard, for whom dreaming up ways to annoy me comes high on the list of priorities, sent Robin off to investigate some squalid little murder in the mud flats of Essex. This called for a drastic change of strategy, for I had been relying on him for an unbiased opinion of his prospective cousin-in-law, and also to keep the temperature down if my own should prove adverse, and a whole evening at home with just the three of us was too daunting to contemplate.

Fortunately I was able to wangle the house seats for a play which had just opened to rave notices, and I booked a table for supper afterwards at a dining club, having first ascertained from the secretary that Jeremy was not a member, so as to avoid any nonsense about who was paying the bill.

Aware of Ellen's predilection for lame ducks, if not hopeless cases, I had resigned myself to meeting someone either shaggy and tongue-tied or bombastically intellectual and even, if pushed, to finding some good in these qualities. Jeremy, however, did not possess them.

We met in the foyer, where he and Ellen had arrived ahead of time, punctuality being one of his unexpected virtues, and I took an instant dislike to him for the very unfair reason that, even before being introduced, he managed to upset all my preconceived theories, so forcing me to abandon the prepared role and adopt a completely opposite approach. Unlike the raffish types I had grown accustomed to through similar encounters, Jeremy was tall and clean shaven and wore an impeccable dark suit and an Old Harrovian tie. He looked as sleek as any successful businessman and, while I have nothing against such people, I associate them more easily with middle age than the early twenties.

The initial hostility was modified after we had gone to our seats, still with ten minutes to wait for curtain up, for I discovered that he had excellent manners, had troubled to acquaint himself with various details about my career and Robin's and could talk with at least superficial intelligence and humour on a number of subjects. Why these qualities should have appealed to Ellen remained as great a mystery as ever, but my own dithering about from one attitude to another was to be the keynote for the evening. At one moment I was admiring his self-assurance and acuteness and in the next the self-assurance struck me as verging on complacency and the conceited tilt of his head was grating on my nerves like the scrape of a knife on china.

During the second interval, having failed to entice us into another struggle to the bar, he went out on his own and Ellen moved up a place and said:

'He's being tactful. Giving you a chance to tell me what you think of him.'

'It's a bit early to judge. He's certainly very bright, and very good-looking.'

'Is that the best you can do?'

'They were meant to be compliments.'

'You didn't make them sound like it.'

'Well, how can one form any sort of opinion in so short a time? Specially with someone like that.'

'Like what?'

'Well, smooth. You have to admit that?'

'No, I don't. It's only that he's going flat out to impress you.'

'Honestly, Ellen, you'll be telling me next that he's a shy, timid fawn, putting on a big act.'

'Yes, I will. Not that I blame you, Tess, because I got just the same first impression myself, but he's not half so confident as he makes out. Anyway, do please make an effort to like him.'

It was an appeal to break down the toughest opposition, but at the time I could only nod and smile, because the exit doors were closing and Jeremy was coming back to his seat, threading his way carefully through the line of knees and ankles and meticulously apologising to each individual as he passed. It was entirely consistent with the picture I had thus far formed of him, for one could neither fault the performance nor repress the thought that none of it would have been necessary if he had bothered to return to his seat a minute earlier.

The same pattern was repeated during dinner and was highlighted when it came to ordering the wine. I had asked him to take charge of this and he did so in an impressively knowledgeable, yet unassuming way, then promptly ruined the effect by recounting a dreadfully patronising anecdote about some pretentious ignoramus making a fool of himself with a *sommelier*.

The final paradoxical note was struck almost at the end, just after I had referred to his and Ellen's horoscopes and had congratulated them on Jezebel's findings. To my surprise, Jeremy did not accept these remarks with his customary complacency but turned very red and stared down at his plate, mumbling something pompous and irritable about hoping to have a more substantial basis for their relationship than that.

Fortunately for my good resolutions, it was possible to attribute this lapse in part to the fact that two women had just entered the restaurant and were making heavy weather of shoving their way past our table. Ellen and I were sharing the *banquette* seat, facing the room, but Jeremy had his back to it and so was taking the brunt of their onslaught and I noticed that one of them actually placed her hand on the back of his chair, tilting it as she went by, so that he was jerked forward and the spoon slithered out of his hand and fell on the tablecloth.

Startled by this gratuitous rudeness, I craned my head to get a closer look at the woman, but she had moved on at a swift clip and all I could tell was that she was exceptionally tall, not less than six feet, with an arrogant and self-conscious bearing and that she had a mass of pale blonde hair piled into a bun at the back of her neck which, against all the known odds, did not make her look in the least dowdy. The next minute she and her companion had disappeared into another *banquette* seat further up the room and out of sight.

It had been a trivial enough incident, but Jeremy never wholly recovered from it. He became steadily more morose and nervous, constantly shifting his chair and plainly paying small attention to anything Ellen and I were saying. We were eventually obliged to fall back on chatting to each other, my estimation of him gradually dropping from five out of ten to zero.

Luckily the point had been reached where I was soon able to ask for the bill, so this tiresome climax to the evening was not prolonged above ten minutes. Moreover, he rallied a little at the end, when we emerged on to the street, thanking me profusely and offering to drive me home. However, both he and Ellen lived in the opposite direction to mine, and nearer to where his car was parked, so it was not difficult to decline. Cutting the argument short, I hurled myself at a cruising taxi and was driven back to Beacon Square, out of temper, out of patience and weighed down by a depressing sense of failure.

CHAPTER FOUR

NEEDLESS to say, Ellen succeeded in charming everyone into the belief that her way was theirs, even soothing away Toby's terror and dismay at the prospect of a marquee with a hundred people inside it, not to mention the deep opposition of Mr Parkes, the gardener, who had visions of his cherished lawn being churned up into a battlefield. The date was fixed for May 26th and Toby promptly handed me an invitation to stay with him for the three days preceding it which I, being between jobs and with two weeks out before the start of rehearsals, had neither wish nor reason to decline. Ostensibly I was there to protect him from telephone callers, caterers, reporters and other sadists whom he visualised queueing up to torment him. It is probable though that my presence was made even more desirable by the fact that, in occupying at least one of the available bedrooms, I should reduce the risk of his having the house swarming with strangers, but I had no doubt that I should be called upon to perform the subsidiary duties as well.

He need not have worried, however, for Ellen, having won the major battle, was careful not to exasperate him further and announced that she would be coming down on her own on the eve of the wedding and that the entire Roxburgh contingent, including two child bridesmaids with their parents and nannies, had engaged rooms at the Swan at Stadhampton. She had also arranged for Jeremy and his brother Simon, who was to be the best man, to spend the night with friends in the village named Roper, and the only concession she asked was that Jeremy's parents, who were driving her down from London, should be received with light refreshments and a civil welcome.

I was faintly taken aback by her choice of Alison Roper's house for it was well known that her son, Phil, was in the top league of Ellen's admirers and had taken the news of her engagement to Jeremy very hard. Since Alison had a somewhat overdeveloped, not to say over-vociferous, maternal instinct, I had expected relations in that quarter to be somewhat cool.

Alison and her children, who included an elder son and daughter, both now married and far away, had come to live at Roakes when her husband bolted with a beautiful Indonesian and she could no longer afford to keep up their house in Hampstead Garden Suburb. She and Toby had never progressed beyond the point of armed neutrality, largely because he was antisocial to an almost paranoiac degree and suffered from the delusion that all widows and divorcées had been put on this earth purposely to torment, bully and, in extreme cases, ensnare him into marriage.

Philip and Ellen, on the other hand, two lonely, one-parent children and more or less of an age, had quickly become allies and, to my certain knowledge, had been engaged to marry each other several times in their early teens. Alison had worked hard at encouraging the friendship and, with typical naivety, had pinned great hopes on its developing into a more enduring relationship. The first blow to these had come when Ellen removed herself to London and took up with the actor, Desmond Davidson, a digression which Alison chose to dismiss, and rightly as it turned out, as no more than a passing phase.

Ellen having now decided to avail herself of Alison's hospitality, I concluded that she assumed Phil's feelings to have been as ephemeral as her own and had taken his dogged and doglike devotion for a mere token of brotherly affection, or else that, aware of the laceration to his feelings in having to share the same roof with her future husband, the need to placate Toby overcame all other scruples.

'Or maybe Phil is getting over his hopeless passion and has found himself a new girl?' I suggested. 'I haven't seen him for months so that could have happened and, if so, all is forgiven.'

This was on Wednesday afternoon, the first of my stay at Roakes Common and Toby and I were idling it away in his revolving summerhouse which, on a principle akin to that of a child closing its eyes in order to become invisible, had been revolved to the position where it backed on to the house and garden, so that nothing could be seen but woods and fields.

'He may have, for all I know. This place he goes to is one of those co-educational affairs, so it is quite likely.'

'You refer to Reading University?'

'That's the one.'

'Propinquity is not everything, Toby.'

'It will have to be, in Phil's case, for it strikes me as highly unlikely that Ellen will alter her arrangements just to accommodate him. In fact, having gone so far, I should think it might be even more bother to cancel them. Besides . . .'

'What?'

'Much as I deplore these Roxburghs, I should feel even more put upon if she were to marry Phil Roper.'

'Oh, he's not a bad boy. Not very polished, I admit, but at least one knows where one is with him.'

'Yes, one does,' Toby agreed. 'Only too well. Living as close as they do, he and his unattractive mother would be round this house like flies. At least the Roxburghs won't be camped on our doorstep.'

'Leaving aside your own prejudices for a moment, you don't think Ellen might have been happier with Phil?'

'Certainly not. He's become a very humourless, moody sort of creature and taken up animal husbandry now, so they tell me. That wouldn't be very thrilling for her.'

'I thought he was reading economics?'

'Perhaps he was, but it all proved too much for him, I suppose. He switched over in his second year. Always a bad sign.'

'Of what?'

'Shilly-shally. It would drive Ellen mad if he were to change his mind every two seconds. I suppose we can rely on Jeremy to be fairly consistent in that way?'

'I don't think he's likely to switch to animal husbandry, if that's what's bothering you, but unsteadiness can take other forms as well, you know. You've seen more of him than I have, but it seems to me that most of the time he's putting on some kind of act. The trouble is that I haven't yet discovered which is the real Jeremy and which is the act; or, come to that, which one Ellen has fallen for. Is she in love with the moody blues character or the suave embryo tycoon, is the question I ask myself?'

'It rather plagues me too, but at least it sounds as though she won't be bored,' Toby said, in the tone of one who rated this among life's major perils.

'She may have other troubles to contend with, though.'

'Most people do, but I assume from these heavy-handed hints that you have something special in mind?'

'What about a discarded mistress, for a start?'

'If she's been discarded, I foresee no bother at all.'

'Then you're an optimist because she's been discarded against her will and is passionately jealous and neurotic.'

'You fascinate me, Tessa! Do go on!'

I was quite willing to, for I had been pondering on the strange encounter with the blonde woman in the dining club, and how it had seemed to coincide with or possibly set off Jeremy's boorish mood and had arrived at the solution that she could only have been Imogen and that shoving the chair forward had been a deliberate act of malice. I was about to describe the incident to Toby and get his views, but was forestalled by the arrival of Mrs Parkes, the housekeeper, wearing a snow white overall and immaculate bouffant hair style. In her hand was a slip of paper with 'Don't Forget' printed across the top in red capitals.

'Sorry to interrupt your lazy afternoon,' she announced, not sounding it. 'This just came through on the phone.

Hope I've got it down right. Some people must have money to burn.'

Toby glanced down at the last line before reading the message, which he did very slowly and then handed it to me, having grown old and grey in the process. It read as follows:

'Why no letter query have just seen press announcement stop love and congratulations to all stop Osgood unfortunately tied up this end but sends greetings stop arriving BA two three nine ex Ottawa fifteen hours your time Friday stop love Irene.'

CHAPTER FIVE

'IT'S A real shocker!' Alison Roper said, snipping ferociously at the dead heads in her herbaceous border. 'A right scandal, if you want my opinion.'

She was a large, mud-coloured, muscular sort of woman, who prided herself on her outspokenness and who had an irritating habit of using slang expressions which she imagined to be up to the minute for her son's generation, although generally lagging several years behind and misapplying them when she did catch up. As it happened, her opinion was the last thing I wanted, for it was invariably in direct conflict with my own, but the delicacy of my mission made it essential not to cross swords with her in the opening round, so I said nothing and she went on:

'I mean, just think of it, Tessa! She's only a kid still, isn't she?'

'Nineteen; and lots of girls get married at that age and make a go of it.'

'I couldn't care less about other girls. My argument is this,' she said, pointing the secateurs at my nose in a slightly threatening manner, 'it's all very fine to marry at nineteen if you've known the chap for years and have an idea what you're letting yourself in for, but Ellen doesn't. How could she? Answer me that!'

Bitterness, self-pity and the grinding struggle to bring up three children single-handed had no doubt helped to make Alison so bossy and aggressive, but sadly enough any direct contact with her merely increased my sympathy with Toby's views. So it was all the more regrettable that he and Ellen, having already wrung one big favour from her, should now have delegated me to beg an even greater one.

'I'm not sure if I can,' I admitted, 'but before I forget what I came for, Toby wants to know if you and Phil will come across for a drink with us on Friday evening. The Roxburghs are bringing Ellen down and since you're being so very kind as to put their son up for the night he thought it would be a nice idea for you all to meet.'

This was a slight paraphrase of my terms of reference, but I was all for seeing what a little conciliation could do to smooth the troubled waters. Not much, as it turned out.

'Oh, he can be very soft soap when he chooses,' Alison said, literally tossing her head, so that she nipped off a perfectly good lupin by mistake. 'That's your Toby all over. Always thinks he can get round people by laying on a bit of the old charm, when it suits him, but it doesn't fool me. He's selfish to the core underneath. Yes, I know you're his cousin and you always stick up for him, but it's time

someone had the guts to say these things. Imagine pushing that poor kid into marriage with the first rich young
man who comes along, just to suit his own convenience!'

This was so far wide of the mark that I was provoked
against my better judgement into argument.

'No, you're all wrong, Alison. This is entirely Ellen's
decision and no one has pushed her into anything. The
truth is that Toby's fairly distraught about it. The last
thing on earth he wants is to lose her, specially to someone he hardly knows and doesn't much care for, but it's
precisely for that reason that he won't interfere. He's so
terrified of being influenced by his own prejudices that
he's tipping over backwards to stay neutral.'

'That's your story, my dear, and you stick to it if it gives
you any joy, but there are those of us who know better.'

'Then you do him an injustice, I promise you, Alison.'
She gave me a patronising smile. 'Quite the little innocent, aren't we? And there's me thinking all you stage
folk are so worldly wise! Still, I suppose it's life which
teaches one the really valuable lessons and I've seen too
much of it to be taken in by your cousin, believe you me!'

'All the same, I hope it won't stop your coming over
to have a drink under his roof on Friday evening?' I
said, in as humble a voice as I could manage, for I had
still not broached the main object of my visit and was
bent on maintaining diplomatic relations until this had
been achieved.

'Oh yes, since his lordship has been so gracious as to
invite us. Can't speak for Phil, of course, but he usually gets
home earlyish on a Friday. That's the advantage of being
so near. He could have got into Oxford or Cambridge, you
know, if he'd wanted to, but he plumped for Reading, so

that he could get over at weekends and be company for his old Mum.'

'That's nice! Has he got a car now?'

'If you can call it that. Old jalopy, really, but it goes at a fairish lick. I suppose young Mr Roxburgh owns a Bentley or a Rolls, doesn't he?'

'No, some fairly ordinary red sports thing, as far as I remember. Quite modest.'

'Not compared to Phil's job, you can bet on that. He bought the old Mini for thirty quid and patched it up himself to get through the M.o.T. Brakes, steering, you name it! It's been a blessing too, now that my old bus has had to be thrown on the scrap heap.'

'Oh no, Alison, you can't mean it? How on earth do you manage up here without a car?'

'Oh, we get by. Phil does a big weekend shopping for me at Stadhampton and I'm used to walking, you know. Still got the use of my legs, whatever else. If I do need a car for special occasions I hire one from Fairman's. He's pretty reliable, on the whole, and what with the tax and insurance and all, it works out cheaper than owning one. What time do you want us on Friday?'

'Six-thirtyish, if that suits you. Oh, by the way, Alison, slight change of plan,' I added, as though struck by an afterthought. 'We've had a cable from Ellen's mother to say she's coming over for the wedding. Could you possibly do a swap and have her to stay instead of the best man?'

'S'pose so,' Alison replied, pushing a grimy hand through her cropped grey hair. 'It'll mean giving her the spare room and doubling Master Jeremy up with Phil. Still, it won't do him any harm to see how the other half lives. What's the catch, though? She'd be a lot more comfortable at Toby's than in our humble abode.'

I debated whether to spin some yarn about Toby's having doubts as to the propriety of his ex-wife staying in the house, but decided this was too far fetched even for Alison to swallow and gambled on the truth instead.

'The fact is, Toby can't stand the sight of her. She ran off with her Canadian husband when Ellen was a baby and he's never forgiven her. I tried to get her a room at the Swan, but they're full up from attic to cellar and quite honestly I think Ellen's last evening at home would be a misery, with both her parents there.'

It paid off, for the gleam in Alison's eye signified that no untruth could have gone down half so well, although it was probably the first part of my confession which had done the trick. Anyone whom Toby couldn't stand the sight of automatically moved up a few notches in Alison's estimation, and she may have felt too that a woman who had abandoned her home and husband for another man had done her share to even the score. Whatever the motive, she acceded with more than her customary grace and I returned to the summerhouse to report on the full success of my mission.

CHAPTER SIX

1

THE grey Rolls-Royce swayed very slowly along the stony track across the common, exuding disapproval from every gleaming panel, and came to rest at Toby's gate. Only Ellen and the chauffeur got out, the latter carrying two large white cardboard boxes, which he laid reverently on the hall table, before pulling the forelock and returning to his place behind the wheel.

'They're going on to lunch with some people near Banbury,' Ellen explained. 'I was invited, but I thought it would be more fun to spend the afternoon with you and Pa.'

'More fun for us too, but they'll be back this evening?'

'Oh yes, no getting out of that macabre little festivity. Six-thirty on the dot, but they won't stay long.'

'Is this all your luggage?' I asked, picking up the second box and following her upstairs.

'Yes, I keep a mass of stuff down here, you see, and my suitcases for tomorrow are already in Jeremy's car. He's still in London, but he'll try and get away by three. I told him to come straight here because he's picking up some presents which people have been sending to the flat. I haven't even had time to open them all yet and I dread to think what Caspar could do if he got his sticky hands on them. Mix up all the cards, for a start. All I've brought with me are my dress and my going away clothes.'

'What about your hair? You'll be mistaken for one of the younger bridesmaids if you wear it like that. Is some-one coming to do it?'

'No, I'll wash it tonight and put it up in the morning. I've been practising in secret, so I know just how to do it and it puts years on me, just you wait and see! I'm a bit bothered about my dress though. It still looks lopsided to me. I thought we might have a trying-on session this afternoon, if you've got time?'

'Well . . .'

'Not if it's a bore,' she said, removing the white dress from its froth of tissue paper and holding it up for my inspection.

'It's not that, but the problem is that Toby has given me the job of collecting your mother from the airport.'

'What a nerve! Why doesn't he order a taxi?'

'I think he feels he can rely on me to drive all the way from Heathrow at two miles an hour, possibly making a detour round Reading, and thus postpone the dreaded moment.'

'Is she coming here, then? I thought you'd loaded her on to poor old Alison?'

'I have, but they've never even met and I thought it would be only civil to bring her here first, to get her bearings. We'll fill her up with soft words and champagne cocktails and Alison can remove her at half-past seven.'

'God, what a nightmare, isn't it?' Ellen asked. 'If only people knew what weddings really involved I am sure the custom would have died out centuries ago.'

I glanced at her curiously but she had spoken in a placid, abstracted kind of way, while holding the dress up against herself and appraising the reflection in the long glass, and hardly appeared to be listening to her own words, much less taking them seriously; so I said,

'I'll go and telephone Owen the taxi and see if he can deputise for me at the airport.'

To which she replied in the same absent-minded strain,

'Brilliant idea, you're a genius! By the way, is Phil coming over this evening?'

'Apparently, he is.'

'Oh, good!'

'You're pleased?'

'Why ever not? We've always got on fine, Phil and me. He's practically my best friend, next to you and Jez, and I'd hate him to feel left out. Besides, I want him to meet Jeremy's father. I think he could be useful and I'm hoping to prevail on him to give Phil a job when he's got his degree. He deserves a break, poor old Phil, and Alison too; and I mean to see they get one.'

It occurred to me as I went downstairs to the hall to telephone that Ellen showed no sign of running out of eccentric reasons for marrying into the Roxburgh clan, but at least she had not so far claimed to be doing so for the sake of Desmond's career, which was perhaps something to be thankful for.

2

Presumably Toby had not been hoping for a major disaster, which must have affected innocent people as well, but he had certainly been keeping his fingers crossed all day that Irene would have changed her mind, missed her plane, or, at the very least, been diverted to somewhere inaccessible like Prestwick, and by half-past five it began to look as though one of these prayers had been answered.

'It's nothing for transatlantic flights to be an hour late, Toby,' and 'It can take ages and ages to get through customs,' Ellen and I reminded him with the utmost regularity, occasionally swapping lines to vary the monotony of our efforts to dampen premature hopes, but his confidence was seen to soar with each repetition of the counterblast:

'Owen would have telephoned by now if there had been something of that nature to account for it.'

'Well, why hasn't he done so in any case?' Ellen demanded when it came out for the third time.

'Obviously, because he is afraid to desert his post. As I see it, what has happened is this: he arrives at the terminal, learns that the plane has landed on time and stations himself near the customs exit, holding up the card with her name on it until his poor old arms are practically dropping off, but still no one approaches. What should he do? No doubt, the suspicion grows, as it does with us, that she was never on the plane at all, but how can he be sure? What if she has passed out in the ladies' cloakroom, or has mislaid her jewel case and is raising hell up and down the building? What should we say to him if, having deserted his post to telephone us, she then came bouncing out and found no one to meet her? Those must be the thoughts which have been chasing through his mind.'

'More likely sitting on the M4 listening to Irene's flow of obscenities because he's had a puncture or run out of petrol.'

'Most improbable,' Toby said, utterly dismissing an explanation which offered so short a reprieve. 'Owen always carries a spare tyre and very likely a spare gallon as well. Besides, the M4 is festooned with telephones every yard of the way.'

However, when at last Owen did ring up, which was not until some further time had gone by and optimism had soared to euphoric heights, his explanation for the delay was far more dramatic than any which had occurred to us, but before this happened we had been joined by Jeremy, who, in this season of shocks and setbacks, had provided his full quota.

He too had arrived late, which was most unlike him, and poor Ellen nearly got her head snapped off when she asked if it had been a tiresome journey.

'That, my darling, is the understatement of the century. How long since you tried getting out of London on a Friday afternoon in full summer? The entire bloody population apparently had the same idea and, so far as I could tell, they were all heading for Stadhampton, though one finds it difficult to understand why.'

'What a shame you couldn't have made an earlier start,' she replied, sounding quite unmoved.

'Wasn't it? Unfortunately, as you may recall, I was obliged to stop off at your flat and collect some parcels.'

'Well, that shouldn't have taken you long.'

'I agree, it shouldn't. Nevertheless, it delayed me by at least half-an-hour. Ten minutes slipped away, if you can so describe it, with me marooned outside the front door, keeping up a three-way conversation with Jez and dear little Caspar. It seems he had locked the mortice and then lost or hidden the key. She was trying to get him to do a total recall, while at the same time keeping up a running commentary for my benefit. I'd have strangled them both, if I could have got at them.'

Ellen sighed. 'Yes, I know, Jez told me. He really is getting to be the end, that Caspar. Never mind, you're here now, so we can all relax.'

Apparently, we couldn't, though, for Jeremy, who had had his tea cup half way to his face, stopped in midstream, then, carefully replacing it said in a frozen voice: 'How do you mean "Jez told you"?'

'Oh, when I rang up. What time was that, Tess? About three?'

'Somewhere around,' I said.

'I'd left my address book in London, you see, and I wanted you to bring it down with the other things, but Jez said you'd already left.'

'At three o'clock? She must be raving! It was after three when I got there.'

'Oh well, I expect she got in a muddle, or perhaps it was later than I thought. Anyway, it doesn't matter a bit because she's promised to bring the book down with her tomorrow. So I'll be able to spend my honeymoon writing postcards, after all,' Ellen said, with such a ravishing smile that I could practically hear the atmosphere crackle and I was glad to see that Jeremy was not impervious to it. He now looked as though he had been poleaxed and was rather enjoying the experience.

'Come on,' she said, instantly turning practical again. 'If you've finished your tea, let's go for a stroll across the common and we'll get you introduced to your hostess.'

He stood up, as docilely as one under hypnosis, then opened the door for her, bending forward to kiss the top of her head as she passed.

It was at this point that the telephone rang, bringing our first news of Irene.

3

'That was Owen on the telephone,' I informed Toby about ten minutes later. 'And the news, from your point of view, is all bad. Irene will be descending on Roakes at any moment. She is somewhat shaken, but alive and well.'

'Shaken?' he repeated, clutching at the only straw in this doleful bulletin.

'She has had an unfortunate experience. They both have.'

'You mean an accident? On the motorway?'

'No, after they'd left it. Owen was speaking from a call box on the Reading-Stadhampton road. He had just left the scene. He couldn't let us know before because he had to wait for the police to come and take over.'

'Take over what?'

'Well, it happened as they were coming down Poynters Hill, you know, where the golf club is? At the top of the hill Owen changed into low gear because he knows all the hazards so well and wasn't taking any chances. It's very steep and there's a fairly sharp curve about half way down and another much more hairpinny one at the bottom.'

'Spare me the topographical survey please, Tessa! I am not a stranger in these parts, you know.'

'Then you'll remember that this hill starts off very deceptively, with quite a gentle, straight slope for the first half-mile and Owen says that at least three cars overtook him at this stage, and all of them going a sight too fast, in his opinion. He wasn't particularly bothered because that road is apt to be rough on Friday evenings with all the traffic streaming out of London.'

'I find all this quite fascinating, but I should still like to know what happened.'

'You're getting it as it came to me and I think it may be important to remember what Owen said, because what we have here is a very nasty hit-and-run thing.'

'Oh dear! Although no one actually hit Irene, I take it?'

'No, but do listen, because Owen has a distinct recollection of one of the cars that passed him then doing some more overtaking and going further up the line, even though they were approaching the first bend by then. Anyway, by the time he got round it himself they were all out of sight and that was when he spotted the child, a boy of about nine or ten, he thinks, and he was spread-eagled on his back against the bank on the left of the road. He could have been asleep, Owen says, only his face was smashed in and there was blood all over the place.'

'Dead?'

'No, still breathing but unconscious, so of course there was no question of moving him, although Owen is pretty sure he was dead by the time the ambulance arrived. On the other hand they couldn't just leave him there while they went to get help, and Irene seems to have been worse than useless. She refused to be left alone with the child, in case he came to and started screaming, and she refused to take the car and find a telephone because she wasn't used to driving on English roads. In fact, Owen admits that it wouldn't have been safe for her to do so because she'd become hysterical by then and was sitting huddled up inside the car, moaning and carrying on like a perfect fool. He was having a pretty hard time all round.'

'I can tell she hasn't changed,' Toby remarked gloomily. 'Go on! Why didn't he stop another car?'

'That was the plan. They'd been flashing past at fairly regular intervals, but not one of them had stopped, or even slowed down. The trouble was that Owen was a bit nervous about stepping out into the road to flag one down, because, coming round that bend, they couldn't see him until they were practically on top of him and he stood a good chance of being the next victim. So anyway, while he was trying to work out what to do and trying to calm Irene down at the same time, he had the most amazing break. A Mini came sailing down the hill and you'll never guess who was driving it.'

'Then I shan't try.'

'Phil Roper, on his way home from Reading for the weekend. Owen doesn't think he meant to stop, any more than the others, but luckily Phil recognised him just in time and pulled up a little further down the hill. So then they arranged that Owen should stay with the child and Phil would drive on to the nearest call box to ring the police, taking Irene with him. He explained that his mother had gone to the dentist in Reading and that he'd promised her faithfully to stop off on his way through Stadhampton and do the weekend shopping for her, but Irene didn't mind that. She didn't mind what happened, so long as she hadn't got to stay there with the child and I think Owen was thankful to be rid of her.'

'That's the only part of the story that doesn't surprise me,' Toby commented. 'Still, one shouldn't be uncharitable, I suppose, and it must have been a hideous shock. Poor woman, how she must wish she had never come!'

Prophetic words, if ever I heard any.

CHAPTER SEVEN

1

THE affianced pair returned, with Irene and Alison in tow, about half-an-hour later, somewhat ahead of the appointed time. Ellen had the explanation.

'Sorry to land them on you so early,' she said, drawing me aside, 'but the fact is that Irene was screeching for a treble Scotch to calm her nerves and, needless to say, there wasn't a drop of anything in the house except beer, so it seemed the only way.'

'Quite all right. It's probably just as well for her to get through the preliminary skirmish with Toby before your in-laws descend on us. Isn't Phil coming?'

'Later, I gather. At least, he'll come and fetch them, which is what matters. I didn't see him, but Alison says he's got an exam tomorrow and was working in his room, and that in any case grand parties aren't much in his line. I can't imagine what she meant.'

'I can. She meant that he's still got the most tremendous crush on you and cannot bear to see you in the Arms of Another.'

'I wouldn't be surprised. She never gives up, that one, but it's all in her imagination, you know. Phil and I get on very well, but he hasn't been faintly in love with me since he was fourteen. What do you think of my mamma? Quite a dish, isn't she?'

'Yes,' I agreed. 'One could say that the years had dealt kindly. Her hair's just as stunning and so is her figure. In fact, when I saw you all walking up the path just now I could have put her down as about twenty-five. The effect isn't quite so good in close-up.'

'More like eighty-five,' Ellen agreed cheerfully. 'She's a monumental bore too, I must warn you.'

Even from a distance of twelve feet, both criticisms could be seen to have some justification. Irene had always been beautiful and neither age nor discontent had blurred the perfect mould of her features and bone structure, but she had the ultra-delicate skin which sometimes goes with red gold hair and, under the enamel make-up, it was puckered and criss-crossed with threadlike wrinkles.

She was wearing a plain, well-cut dark dress, with a high, white ruffled organdie collar, which made a wonderfully becoming frame for her head, but also suggested that the years had caused even worse ravages to her neck. Knowing how ardently she had always worshipped her own beauty, I had begun by feeling a little sorry for her but pity was soon strangled by irritation, for now, as in the past, she was far too talkative and her conversation centred exclusively on herself.

There can be few topics more tedious than other people's aeroplane journeys, and other people's road accidents run them a close second. I probably did not suffer such agonies of boredom over the latter as the rest of her audience, for at least I had the fun of comparing her version with Owen's, in which, far from displaying the coolness and resource she now boasted of, she had remained firmly inside the car, shooting down nerve pills, refusing to cooperate and yelling her head off when requested to do so.

Perhaps she detected a faint smirk in my expression, for I got my come-uppance when I trotted over with her second refill of whisky, her screams of protest that she could tolerate no other beverage having coincided with the popping of the first champagne cork.

'Oh, my dear Tessa, aren't you sweet? What a perfect little waitress you've grown into! And they tell me you're married to a policeman! Can it be true?'

'Yes, quite true.'

'How quaint! But we could certainly have done with him this afternoon, if he had happened to come by on his motor bike. And so you've quite given up the stage, have you?'

This was a backhander and no mistake, because I knew for a fact that at least two of my recent films, as well as a television serial, had been shown in Canada, and furthermore I suspected that Irene knew it too.

'No, indeed she hasn't,' Ellen said, coming rather too vehemently to my defence. 'You couldn't be more mistaken. Tessa's having a very, very great success at present.'

'Hush, darling!' Irene said in a pained voice. 'No need to shout at me! I'm not in Winnipeg now, you know!'

Toby, who had been leaning back in his chair with his eyes closed, now opened them briefly and said, 'We had noticed,' before sliding back into oblivion once more.

With masterly economy, she had managed to get us all on the hop and the one who was enjoying it almost as much as Irene herself was Alison. During the short, uncomfortable silence which followed Toby's comment, she smiled down into her glass of light ale as though sharing a delicious secret with it, in the confident expectation of there being more to come.

It was left to Irene to set the ball rolling again, which she did in her own inimitable fashion by saying with a faint titter:

'A little case of pre-wedding nerves here, I can see. Poor Irene must tread very carefully. Even Jeremy is frowning at me as though I had committed some dreadful sin, though I can't imagine how I could have said anything to upset him.'

Jeremy, who, up till then, had been silent and pudding-faced, now astonished me by entering the fray with all guns firing. Placing a protective arm round Ellen's shoulder, he said,

'My dear Mrs Lewis, you really will have to learn not to underestimate yourself.'

Toby momentarily opened his eyes again and the sudden anger which tightened Irene's mouth showed clearly how all the surrounding lines and wrinkles had got there. Turning to the window to hide my laughter, I was rewarded by the sight of the grey Rolls lumbering towards us over the common. The happy domestic gathering was about to be augmented by the Roxburghs.

2

So far as appearances went, they were a family split down the middle, for Stella Roxburgh was tall and dark, like Jeremy, with the arrogant, faintly disdainful manner which also occasionally manifested itself in him, although I guessed that not even charitable Ellen would have attributed it to shyness on her part. Her height was accentuated by a straight-backed stance and supremely elegant clothes and she was roughly the same width all the way down, from shoulder to knee. I was interested to see that during the round of introductions Irene and I got covertly appraising looks, Alison's presence was acknowledged, without apparently being registered, and her affectionate greeting of Ellen was a mockery compared to the adoring smile she conferred on Jeremy. However, she was far too socially disciplined to go over and talk to him and, dutifully attaching herself to Toby, started boring him to death by extolling the beauties of the countryside.

Her husband, on first acquaintance, was a more endearing and much less formidable character for, except for his nose, which was curved and bony and out of proportion to the rest, he was a chubby, rotund little man, with round blue eyes in a round face and with an engagingly friendly manner and in all these respects Simon, the younger son, resembled him closely.

Arnold, having greeted the whole party with indiscriminate effusiveness, immediately devoted himself to Ellen, although I doubt if his attentions were dictated by any particular social rule. He was obviously a man who enjoyed the company of pretty young women, and Ellen responded very gracefully, seating herself on the arm of his chair and smiling affectionately at his jokes and compliments. Watching them, as I ran round offering drinks and relaying the orders back to Jeremy, who had put himself in charge of the bar, I was uncomfortably reminded of Alison's strictures and found myself wondering how far being treated like the sugar plum fairy and loaded with expensive gifts by her prospective father-in-law might have contributed to a rose-coloured view of his son.

A slightly less disturbing subject of speculation was offered by the sight of Alison and Irene, now engaged in a heart-to-heart chat on the sofa. No two women could have been more unlike and, at best, one could have anticipated a contemptuous indifference on the part of each, but in fact they had achieved a most remarkable *entente*. One possible explanation was that both were being virtually ignored by everyone else in the room and were both intent on accepting defeat gracefully, but Irene possessed little grace and Alison no artifice and I guessed that the cause lay a shade deeper. It was a truism, of course, that Alison was predisposed towards any declared enemy of Toby's, and it also occurred to me now that Irene's hunger for admiration was so insatiable that, as the regular supply dried up, she had become increasingly indiscriminate in tapping other sources and that even plain, dowdy old Alison's esteem was balm of a kind.

In one way it was a most satisfactory development for I knew Toby had been terrified that Irene would expect to be invited to stay on for dinner, whereas all the stars now foretold with one voice that we should have no difficulty in bundling her off with Phil and Alison. Nevertheless, the sight of them so cosy and chirpy for some indefinable reason spelt trouble. Irene was not reputed to be much given to thoughtless impulse and, since her motives were generally destructive, anything at all out of character was bound to arouse misgivings.

Simon was the only guest to be left without occupation of some kind, so I invited him to come upstairs and inspect his room. He was a dapper, twinkly young man, with a puffed up halo of golden hair, somewhat taller than his father, though dwarfed by Jeremy, and with exceptionally small hands and feet. All the same, he lacked any trace of effeminacy and reminded me a little of a portrait I had once seen of P.B. Shelley. On the surface, too, he was a less complicated character than his brother, with a friendly unselfconscious manner, who pounced on all my remarks with an eagerness to suggest that he had never received such polite attention in his life and several times repeated his thanks for putting him up for the night when we must already have such a lot on our plates. Later I was to discover that he used this kind of jargon in a derisory spirit, but at the time I took him seriously and said,

'No, not at all. The caterers are seeing to everything and it all seems to be running very smoothly.'

'Still, I remember so well when my sister got spliced. The Coronation didn't come near it.'

'Well, no doubt this will be a very simple affair by comparison, but I must warn you that inside that pink velvet glove your new sister-in-law conceals a very iron, efficient hand.'

'Does she, by Golly? How delighted I am to hear that! My poor old brother really needs someone to tell him which foot to put in front of the other.'

I was hoping he might elaborate on this remark, but he had strolled over to the window and was gazing out.

'I say, what a superb view we have here over your mature, secluded and well-stocked garden! You are lucky to live in such a rural gem!'

'I don't live in it. At least, only occasionally.'

'No, that's right,' Simon said, turning round again and eyeing me in a speculative fashion. 'You live in London, as I remember, in the purlieus of Scotland Yard, and your husband is a detective. Will he be in attendance at the wedding.'

'He's promised to try.'

'Oh, good! I'm so looking forward to meeting him.'

'There's even a faint chance that he'll get away this evening, but I gather you won't be dining here?'

'Unhappily, no. Well, I don't mean that exactly, but these family functions can be a bit overpowering to sensitive souls like mine. Unfortunately, my mother would have the vapours if the entire clan wasn't gathered together on Jeremy's last evening in the ancestral home. Figuratively speaking, that is. In fact, we'll be gathered in the Swan Hotel. They have quite a commodious private dining room overlooking the river, usually reserved for Rotary luncheons I understand, which has been put at our disposal.'

'Well, it must be nice in a way to be a member of such a united family. Does your sister look like you, or like Jeremy?'

'Which one? I've been blessed with three, you know. Caroline's a bit like me, poor dear; the other two take after my mother.'

'And will they all be with you this evening?'

'You bet! All booted and spurred, and I'll tell you something else to make your flesh creep.'

'What?'

'I have a nasty feeling that my mother will expect me and Jeremy and our captive brother-in-law, who can never have known what he was getting into, to go sneaking off after dinner on some drunken revelry *à la stag*. Not that she approves of heavy drinking in the normal way, you understand?'

'All part of the conventional pre-wedding scene?'

'I say! Jolly quick off the mark, aren't you? That's the ticket, and a fairly macabre one too, I might add, since none of us is particularly keen on pubs and I doubt if Stadhampton has much else to offer in the way of night life.'

'No, but even the pubs close at ten-thirty, so you won't have to spin out your debauchery.'

'Good thinking, Tessa! I may call you Tessa, may I not? I positively feel I've known you for ages. And, between you and me, it may not be such a bad idea to leave the family festive board fairly early.'

'Really? Why's that?'

Feeling that he had known me for ages, Simon barely hesitated before replying,

'The fact is, there was someone at the reception desk when we came out just now. The parents don't even know her by sight, having exhibited the coldest of shoulders, but I met her once or twice in the period when she was hanging around Jeremy and it gave me quite a *frisson*. Up to no good, I said to myself.'

'You wouldn't be referring to a tall and statuesque blonde, by any chance?'

'There now! Nothing much gets past you, does it? Comes of being married to a detective, I dare say. Yes, that's the one all right, good old Imogen. They didn't have a room for her at the Swan, as it happens, but I doubt if a little hitch like that would deter her. She'll find somewhere to doss down, you may be sure, and I expect you agree that it might be a good idea to fling a cordon round old Jeremy for the next twelve hours or so, lest we find ourselves going forward, shoulder to shoulder, straight up the creek.'

CHAPTER EIGHT

1

PROBABLY the most burning question of the hour before any marriage ceremony is the one relating to the weather and, despite some gloomy forecasts on the previous day, Saturday, May 26th dawned soft and shining, with a sunlit haze partially veiling the yellow and white marquee, and the birds singing out their promise of ideal conditions to come.

By nine o'clock the mist had melted, the promise had been fulfilled and the caterers' men were whistling a merry tune as they unloaded their wares from a lorry parked on the common. None of this, however, was any consolation to me at all when word filtered through that we were short of a bridegroom.

Naturally it was Alison who fired the first shot in this round, and never had anyone taken aim more gleefully, although, by a merciful providence, missing her target by several inches.

Her call came through soon after nine, which was unlucky timing from her point of view, because Ellen had asked not to be disturbed before ten and, in a strange reversal of roles, Mrs Parkes was busy doling out tea and biscuits to the caterers. It would not have occurred to Toby to answer the telephone if he had been alone with it on a desert island, which left only myself and, by putting on the performance of a lifetime, I managed to take her down a notch or two with a fine display of nonchalance, even if not wholly convincing her that young men who vanished without a trace on the eve of their weddings were two a penny in smart society.

Having spiked these guns for the nonce, I sped forth in search of the best man and suffered another minor heart attack when it transpired that the spare room was empty. However, there was no question about his bed having been slept in and two minutes later I ran him to earth in the dining room. He was wearing a dressing gown over pyjamas and was wolfing down his cornflakes, apparently without a care in the world.

'When did you last see your brother?' I demanded, ignoring his breezy salutation.

'You should only ask that question when you're wearing your blue silk knee breeches and long golden curls,' he replied reprovingly, and then added, 'Last night when he dropped me off here. Why?'

'The time being?'

'About eleven, give or take. You were right about the pubs. You didn't hear me come in? That was because I crept upstairs as quiet as a tight little mouse.'

'What did Jeremy do after that?'

'Snuggled into bed like me, I suppose. What else?'

'Did he actually tell you he was going to do that?'

'I don't know that he did. There wouldn't have been any reason to. We passed the house on the way here and he pointed it out to me, so he can hardly have got lost.'

'Nevertheless, he did get lost.'

'I wish you'd elucidate, Madam.'

'He either lost his way to the Ropers, or he never intended to go there, but either way he didn't turn up. Alison rang five minutes ago to report. They all went to bed early too, because Irene was tired out by her journey and Jeremy had his own key. Phil sat up working for a while in his room and as there was still no sign of Jeremy when he packed it in at around midnight he assumed he was having a night on the Stadhampton tiles. That's all he knew until his mother called him half an hour ago and they discovered the other bed hadn't been slept in. What construction are we to put on that?'

'I'm baffled, frankly.'

'He couldn't have changed his mind and spent the night at the hotel?'

'Rather eccentric, wouldn't you say, since your friends were expecting him? I suppose it has to be the answer, though, and I must regretfully assume that the poor old boy has gone out of his mind. I will not make any secret of the fact that the principal reason for getting Ellen to fix us up in lodgings with the local gentry was to place ourselves outside the maternal net on this of all days. My mother means well, but in jollifications of this nature she is apt to take on the characteristics of an over-protective steamroller.'

'You wouldn't feel inclined to ring her up now and see if Jeremy is there?'

'With respect, I think that's a poisonous idea. If he is there, she'll get him to the church on time, so we need have no worries on that score; whereas, if he's not, she'll go rather noisily off her head.'

'In addition to which, there could be another explanation, couldn't there?'

'Which hovers between us like a menacing cloud. I agree, but, in that case, least said soonest mended, perhaps?'

'I honestly don't know,' I confessed. 'You appear to be taking it all very calmly, but how can we be sure that he intends to come back? Do you realise that in precisely half-an-hour I have to call Ellen and start helping her to dress? Not a very enviable task, considering that the bridegroom may even now be on his way to Majorca with his ex-mistress.'

Simon shook his head. 'Most improbable. In the first place, having once got shot of her, nothing on earth would induce him to go back. In the second, he happens to be potty about Ellen and asks nothing more than to cleave only unto her.'

'I just hope you're right, that's all.'

'You may depend upon it. Providing he's alive, he'll be waiting at the church when Ellen floats in, come hell or high water.'

'None of which helps to solve the problem of what he's up to at this moment.'

'Oh, he may have some final little bachelor business to settle, who can say? He can be very cagey at times, just like my father. He has his own way of going about things and he doesn't always choose to tell us what they are.'

'So your advice would be to sit tight, say nothing and keep our fingers crossed?'

'I should think that would do nicely, so far as you are concerned, but personally I have a more active role in mind. I can at least plug up one hole. What's your friend's name? Hooper?'

'Roper. Alison Roper. What will you say to her?'

'Oh, I shall concoct some little tale while I make my toilette,' Simon said, tightening his dressing gown cord in the manner of one literally girding up his loins. 'Something about Jeremy having mislaid his key during last night's rough and tumble, and of fearing to disturb them and so on and so forth.'

'Well, we don't stand on ceremony, you know. You are not required to dress before using the telephone.'

'Telephoning doesn't come into it; I mean to hasten there in person. In that way, I shall be on the spot when Jeremy returns and we can avoid the embarrassment of conflicting explanations. Also, if I mooch about, getting under Mrs Roper's feet and offering to help her with little jobs around the house, I may conceivably impede her from spreading the story round the entire neighbourhood, which is the first essential. So be of good cheer and let us go forward together, undismayed.'

'Smart thinking!' I told him. 'And I owe you an apology.'

'For what, Madam?'

'Yesterday I put you down as one of those flighty types who would either lose the ring or turn up at the wrong church, but I take it all back. I really do think you're probably the best man for the job.'

2

The front door was open as Simon and I bustled through the hall on our separate errands, and a dreamy, ethereal figure, with long flaxen hair flowing over a white candle-wick dressing-gown, came wafting in from the garden.

'Where the hell have you been?' I demanded, coming to a dead stop.

'Walking on the common.'

'In your dressing gown?'

'Why not? I'm perfectly decent, aren't I?' she enquired, glancing down at her knees to verify the fact.

'Perfectly decent and ever so stunning,' Simon told her. 'All the same, I'm bound to feel thankful that my mother wasn't here to see.'

'I thought you meant to sleep until ten?' I said.

'I know, but I woke up, you see, and it was such a heavenly blissful morning that I was inspired to take a last nostalgic stroll. It reminded me of all the walks we used to have on the common when I was a child, and before you married Robin, and it was all so sad and beautiful that I began to cry. So there I was, sitting on that huge enormous tree trunk we used to call Arthur's throne, crying away like mad.'

'You don't look as though you've been crying,' I informed her. 'You look rather cheerful.'

'Oh, I am, because the most extraordinary and miraculous thing happened. There I was, all alone and wallowing in sentiment, when along came Jeremy.'

'You don't say!'

'Yes, I do, and so then of course I stopped crying and everything was all right again. Can you imagine anything more romantic?'

'What was Jeremy doing on the common at that hour? Had he been out all night?'

'No, of course not, what a daft idea! He was like me, he woke early and thought it would be fun to go for a walk. Wasn't it super that we should both have had the same idea? You see, Jez was quite right about us! I suppose you couldn't be twenty angels, Tess, and rustle up some breakfast? All this exercise and emotion has given me a furious appetite.'

She had floated across to the staircase by this time and I said casually,

'I'll apply myself to it right away. Did Jeremy tell you how long he'd been out when you met him?'

'No, but it must have been quite a while because he'd already been to the garage.'

'Garage? What garage?'

'There is only one, isn't there? It's called Fairman's, but it belongs to Owen's brother. You know, up by the Bricklayers' Arms.'

'What did he want to go there for?'

'To get his car fixed. Why else would one go to a garage? I hope you haven't forgotten that I'm starving?'

'Yes, all right, but you see, Ellen, Alison rang up just now and she was in a bit of a tizz at finding Jeremy had already gone out when she went to call him. Simon and I have been wondering about it.'

'Oh, she is a fusspot, that Alison! No wonder it gets Phil down sometimes. Anyway, you can all stop worrying now because what happened was that Jeremy woke up early, just like me, and decided to go for a walk. Well, for one thing, Phil was snoring like a bull, so there wasn't a chance of going to sleep again. So he flung on some clothes and went downstairs.'

'Yes, but how did Fairman's garage creep into the script?'

'I'm coming to that. You see, his first idea was to go for a drive, but when he took his car out he was disturbed to find that it had had a nasty biff.'

'Oh really? What kind of biff?'

'Like someone must have backed into him when they were parking. The bumper was bent and one of the headlights was on the skew.'

'When did all that happen?'

'No knowing, but he thinks it can only have been when it was outside the hotel during dinner. Anyway, it can't have happened later than that.'

'Why not?'

'Because Phil had very sweetly told him to put it away in the garage. The forecast had said rain and Phil said it wouldn't matter nearly so much if his own car got wet; but the point is that Jeremy was terribly put out when he saw the damage because we've got to drive over to Newhaven this evening and put it on the ferry and it would be rather shaming if the headlight fell off before we'd even got half way there. So he had the bright idea of taking it up to Fairman's and getting them to work on it. Luckily, they open at eight and there was no problem at all. They've promised to fix it and deliver it back to him by eleven. Plenty of time for you both to get to the church,' she added, smiling at Simon, who was looking curiously thoughtful, 'And now, if the inquisition is over, could I remind you that people are supposed to be humoured on their wedding day and the thing to humour me most at this moment would be a whacking great plate of sausages and bacon.'

'What do you make of that?' I asked Simon when Ellen had drifted away upstairs and out of sight.

'I think it will do very nicely,' he replied. 'Very nicely indeed. I'm surprised I didn't think of it myself.'

'Was there anything wrong with the headlamp when you drove up here last night?'

'Well, I couldn't readily swear that I was in a fit state to notice. Besides, what's the odds? The great thing is that he's safely back in harbour and not for us to hazard a guess about any rough passages he may have encountered on the way. Just for once, I fancy the idea of leaving every stone in place and going forward together with our blinkers on.'

Nevertheless, some nagging doubts still lingered and, to my surprise, as I stood turning sausages over in a pan and thoughts in my mind, the most obstinate of these was in a sense the most trivial. With the best will in the world, I could not associate Jeremy with the kind of considerate young man who, having risen early to go for a drive in the country, would then spare the time to remake his bed so meticulously that to all appearances it had never been slept in.

3

The only minor turbulence to shatter the calm of the next two hours centred on the problem of who was to convey Simon from our house to the Ropers', where he was to present himself and take charge of the bridegroom on the stroke of eleven. I was unable to leave Ellen at this crucial stage, Toby flatly refused to go, for fear of running into Irene, and Simon was unwilling to incur the ribaldry of the local populace by making the journey on foot, rigged out in striped trousers, morning coat and grey top hat. The solution was eventually provided, with breathtaking simplicity, by Ellen. She advised us to tell the garage to deliver Jeremy's car to us, instead of to its owner. It arrived punctually at ten to eleven, looking as sleek and unscathed as the day it had left the showroom.

It had been arranged that Owen should collect Ellen and Toby exactly one hour later, in his most sedate and sober limousine, and that I should go ahead in Toby's old Mercedes, thus enabling me to remain at my post until the last possible moment; but no programme, however carefully conceived, could be proof against Irene's whims and Simon had not long left us when Alison rang up to report on a new setback. No power on earth, it transpired, would induce Irene to drive to the church in Phil's car.

It was a measure of the astonishing *entente* between the two ladies that Alison took even this aspersion in her stride.

'One does see her point,' she told me. 'Dear old Phil's had a jolly good bash at smartening it up and I must say it looks a treat, but these Minis are a bit tricky to get in and out of, and one couldn't call it the most dignified way for the bride's mother to arrive. That's what she is, you know, even though everyone but me seems to have forgotten it, and I do think that Toby should have made proper provision for her.'

Personally, I could not see how it could possibly matter to anyone, except Irene herself, if she travelled to the church in a handcart but, recognising that I should only waste more time by expressing this view, I said,

'All the same, it's rather late to do anything about it now. You could try ringing Stadhampton for a taxi, but I doubt if you'd get one at such short notice, this being Saturday. Have you any other suggestions?'

'Well, don't be a clot, lass! You've got the Mercedes, haven't you? What's to stop you coming round this way and collecting her yourself?'

'Only that I'd promised to stay with Ellen until the bitter end.'

'Can't see what difference five minutes would make.'

'You know it would take longer than that, Alison. Oh well, never mind, we'll manage somehow. Just tell Irene to be ready by a quarter to twelve, or else. If she isn't, she can walk.'

Having relieved my feelings slightly with this ultimatum, I replaced the receiver and turned to find Toby standing behind me.

'I suppose you caught the gist of that?' I asked. 'Detestable woman! Why does she always have to make everything so complicated?'

'It is the only pleasure left to her. We must be thankful she didn't dream up something twice as difficult to comply with.'

'So you think I should take her with me?'

'It seems the only way and at least you can keep her within bounds. If we send anyone else she'd be sure to keep them waiting and the next thing would be that the service was held up for Irene to make her entrance. No doubt she's already thought of that and it will be up to you to thwart her.'

'How about Ellen, though? It does seem a shame that she should be put out.'

'And when have you known that to happen? She's the last one in the world to be flustered by such a trifle. Thank God, on my knees fasting, there never was a girl who less resembled her mother.'

He was right, of course. Ellen received the news with complete serenity and when I had helped her fix her veil in place and she had reciprocated by tilting my hat one centimetre further forward over my nose, I left her sitting on her bed, reading the correspondence column of *The Times*, her white dress spread out around her and the bouquet of yellow and white roses at her side.

'All set,' I told Toby, descending once more to the hall. 'See you at the barricades!'

CHAPTER NINE

I HAD timed my arrival at the Ropers' for eleven-forty precisely, for I knew that it would be a matter of honour for Irene to keep me waiting a token five minutes and

reckoned that it would be diplomatic to give her the satis-
faction of believing that I was sweating it out in a fever
of nervous tension.

Phil and Alison were just setting off when I drew up,
Alison wearing a dress of some hideous dark green slith-
ery material, which was too tight for her, and a white felt
helmet with a green feather stuck through it like a hatpin,
and Phil sporting a pale tan suit and blue tie. It was the
first time I had seen him for nearly a year and the first
time ever when he had not been wearing shabby jeans
and a tee shirt. The improvement was so impressive that
I tactlessly remarked on it.

'Give over, for goodness sake! You're embarrassing
the poor chap. He feels a right Charlie, as it is,' Alison
said, answering for him as usual.

Phil blushed a fiery scarlet, although whether to under-
line her point or from fury at her making it was not clear.

'Is Irene ready?'

'Just about. She was feeling a bit off colour, first thing,
and we had panic stations at one point because she'd lost
her bag, but it turned up in the downstairs loo, so everything's hunky-dory now. Go and give her a shout, Phil,
there's a good lad.'

'I'm surprised he's consented to come,' I said, watching him lope away. He was a bony, ungainly young man,
whose breadth had not yet caught up with his height and
with a head too small for his shoulders which added to
the general impression of immaturity.

'I had a right old job persuading him,' Alison admitted. 'But I told him that anything was better than moping
at home. The fact is, he's got to face up to the situation
sooner or later so he may as well jump in at the deep end.

The trouble with my old Phil is he's too inclined to bottle things up. You can see it's getting him down though. Right off his food, too. "You won't do any good by starving yourself, my lad," I told him. "That never mended a broken heart." Wouldn't listen, of course. He's the salt of the earth, but . . .'

She rambled on in this strain for a while, but, like Phil, I ceased to listen, for the precious five minutes had almost run out and most of my attention was concentrated on the doorway through which he had vanished. I was debating whether to follow him when Irene emerged on to the porch, a vision of loveliness in a pink and white printed silk dress, with stand-up collar and matching wide-brimmed hat, which shaded her face in the most kindly and becoming way imaginable.

I was mentally rehearsing a few fulsome and flattering comments, with which to boost her vanity and soothe her into an amiable humour on the drive to the church, when all the fearful anxiety which her presence had dispelled came flooding back in double strength. A shadow across the rear mirror had caused me to look up and I saw that a Panda car had stopped behind me. A plain-clothes policeman opened the passenger door and stepped out of it at the precise moment that Irene stopped her teetering progress down the path and stood aside to allow Phil to open the gate for her.

Luckily for me, he fumbled it a bit and in the two or three seconds while he struggled with the latch I was out of the Mercedes and had covered the distance between it and the Panda car.

'Good morning!' I said, making it as brisk and businesslike as I dared. 'Can I help you?'

'Would you be Mrs Irene Lewis, by any chance?'

'No, I wouldn't. Actually, my name is Price.'

'Sergeant Brooks, Madam. This would be Holly Lodge?'

'That's right.'

'I understand you have a Mrs Lewis staying here?'

'Yes, and I think I can guess why you want to see her, but listen, I want to ask you a big favour. Do you think you could possibly come back a little later on? Mrs Lewis's daughter is being married at twelve o'clock. She's come all the way from Canada specially for the occasion and we'll only just be in time if we leave immediately.'

'Oh certainly, in that case I shouldn't wish to detain her, but this won't take more than a minute. Or if I might just have a word and find out what time would be convenient?'

'No, please!' I entreated, throwing everything into it. 'She's very nervous and highly strung and she's already been badly shaken by that awful business yesterday. I'm telling you this in confidence, but we're all a bit worried in case she might have some kind of breakdown. This is a very emotional time for her, you see, but it will all be over by four o'clock and I guarantee to escort her back here personally as soon as her daughter and the bridegroom have left.'

I had kept my voice down as low as possible while reeling off this farrago, for I knew that Irene would leap at the chance of describing her roadside heroism to the sympathetic young policeman, even if it meant holding up the wedding ceremony until midnight, and it may have been the breathless urgency of my tone which lent conviction to the appeal. There was a fractional hesitation and then the sergeant's hand brushed his forehead in a kind of reflex salute, as he said,

'Very good, Madam, I'll return here at five o'clock if you think that's best. I gather from the driver we interviewed on the spot that Mrs Lewis is unlikely to have anything material to add to his account, so there's nothing for her to be alarmed about, but I quite understand that the circumstances are exceptional. Sorry to come barging in at a time like this, but you know how it is?'

'What was all that about?' Alison asked, hitching up her tight skirt, preparatory to crawling into the Mini.

'Nothing important, I'll tell you later. We should all make a dash for it now, or Ellen will arrive before we do. You go ahead, Phil, and then you'll be able to take Irene in. Front pew on the left, don't forget! It doesn't matter about me. I can always hurtle in when I've parked, and sit at the back, if necessary.'

Accustomed to being ordered about by a bossy female, he obeyed without a murmur and shot off down the road, just as the church bells pealed out their first summons. We had exactly ten minutes in hand, which was still enough, so I allowed Irene to take her time in draping herself and her clothes over the passenger seat, and to go through the routine check in the mirror behind the sun shield, only pretending to fume and fidget with impatience, so as to make it more amusing for her, since it all provided Phil with the necessary few minutes to get into position at the receiving end.

'I can't stand church bells,' she complained petulantly as we skimmed along at a steady twenty-five miles an hour. 'So depressing somehow. Toby and I were married at Caxton Hall. It tickles me to think of him putting on a show like this.'

'I don't think he had much choice.'

'No, I expect those Roxburghs organised everything. Pseudo and pretentious to the last! It quite saddens me to think of a child of mine getting into the clutches of that lot!'

'Why's that, Irene? Did you know them before?'

'Not him. At least, Osgood had dealings with him once over some merger or other with a Canadian company. He said Arnold was as tricky as they come. I wouldn't know about that, but Stella and I were girls together in the old days.'

'Really? I had no idea.'

'We were at RADA together. Not in the same year; she's a good bit older than me, but I knew her by sight. Well, everybody did, my dear. Not a type I admire, but striking, you know, even in those days. For all her lower-middle-class gentility, I have to confess she was definitely striking.'

'And talented?' I asked, not displeased to find some of Irene's venom being drained off on such a distant target.

'Devoid, my dear; utterly and totally devoid. She fell back on the other method, if you'll excuse the pun. Queen of the casting couch, if you know what I mean? Still, she's so grand these days that I'm sure she'd hate to be reminded of her unsavoury past, so I must remember to be awfully, awfully discreet. What did that policeman want, by the way?'

This was the question I had been steeling myself for, but as the Panda car, which had trailed us for the first few hundred yards, had now turned off on to the main Dedley road, I felt safe in giving a straight answer:

'As a matter of fact, Irene, he wanted to see you, or rather to find out when it would be convenient to do so.'

'Me? Whatever for? What am I supposed to have done?'

'Nothing, I imagine, beyond getting yourself mixed up in a motor accident. You're a witness, in so far as you bear out Owen's statement that the boy had been knocked down before you got there.'

'Then why the hell couldn't you have said so before and allowed me to speak to him?' she demanded furiously.

'It was hardly the moment to get embroiled in that sort of thing, was it? He's agreed to come back this evening.'

'I must say, my dear, you've grown into a very conceited little busybody, haven't you? I'll thank you to mind your own bloody business in future. I suppose your tiny success has quite gone to your head! It may surprise you to learn that I am not a complete imbecile and perfectly capable of making my own decisions.'

'No, it doesn't, but as you didn't make any move at the time, I thought I was only doing what you'd want. You must have realised it was a police car?'

'Of course I realised it was a police car. I'm not blind either; but it never crossed my mind that they'd come to see me. Naturally, when you went waltzing over to them I concluded it was some friend of your husband's who'd brought you a message. Really, I could slay you for your bloody interference. Now I'll have the horror of it hanging over me for the whole day, instead of being able to relax and enjoy myself.'

The church was now in sight and I could see one or two people still going in. Phil and Alison were in position under the thatched roof over the gate and I said soothingly:

'There's absolutely no reason why you shouldn't relax as much as you like, Irene. All you'll be asked to do is answer a couple of simple questions, just to corroborate Owen's statement, and that'll be that.'

'Oh, you think so, do you?' she asked, flashing her splendid eyes at me as I drew up beside the gate. 'Well, I've news for you, my child. You're not quite so clever as you seem to believe. I have something very interesting to tell that policeman, which may surprise the lot of you. If I choose to, that is,' she added, turning her back on me and climbing out of the car.

CHAPTER TEN

1

IN ACCORDANCE, so I was told, with hallowed tradition, all the flowers had been provided by the bridegroom's parents and here again the motif was monotonously yellow and white. Half a dozen experts had arrived direct from Covent Garden at eight o'clock in the morning, with two vans laden with white roses and white and yellow orchids, and had been working flat out until half-an-hour before zero hour. The result was breathtakingly beautiful and totally inappropriate, as though some multi-millionaire, cheated of his desire to hold a party in the Albert Hall, had transported the entire decor to St Mary's Parish Church.

None of this made more than a passing impression on me as I entered, for my principal concern was with the occupants of the two front pews, where I had the overwhelming relief of seeing Jeremy and Simon seated decorously on the right and, across the aisle from them, the brim of Irene's pink hat bobbing about, as she chatted in animated style to the tall Prince Charming at her side, whose name was Robin Price.

Reluctant to throw a spanner in these well-oiled works by pushing past her, still less to usurp her place of honour next to Toby, I made a detour by way of the side aisle, so as to approach from the rear, and as a result had the disagreeable shock of seeing a solitary and familiar figure crouched in one of the small pews at the back and one, moreover, whom I felt reasonably certain was present without benefit of invitation.

There was no opportunity to pass on my misgivings to Robin because by the time I had edged in beside him the bells had grown silent as the organ tuned up for the first hymn, and the whole congregation was craning round to catch a first glimpse of the bride.

She was followed by a page wearing the inevitable yellow trousers and white frilly shirt and by four prim-looking, matching bridesmaids of assorted ages and, as she looked everything that could possibly be desired by the most critical and sentimental wedding guest plus a bit extra which was all her own, further description would be superfluous.

She was greeted by Jeremy, with a smile compounded of equal parts of dazzlement and awe, both of which looked genuine and Toby, having done his bit part very nicely, retreated to his place beside Irene, without giving her a glance. In fact, on looking back on it, I doubt if he ever glanced at her again from that moment until the end of her life.

So far as I am concerned, once the cast is assembled and the action starts, the only truly gripping moment in the marriage service comes right at the beginning, when the question is thrown out as to whether anyone present knows just cause or impediment, etc. Expertly timed and delivered in an awesome enough tone, this can make for a very tense moment indeed and I have never understood why somewhere, far away in the depths of my mind, there used to lurk a tiny, nonconformist hope that someone actually would stand up and speak now.

It had not happened to me yet and did not do so now, but what occurred next came sufficiently close to the real thing to have killed that particular tiny hope for ever. The regulation pause was nearly up and the vicar had opened his mouth to deliver the next line when there rang out from the back of the church a hoarse and lunatic shriek of laughter, such as would have curdled the blood of any Lyceum audience at the turn of the century and which had pretty much the same effect on the congregation of St Mary's Church.

In the appalled silence which followed almost everyone turned his head or lowered it in disgust and embarrassment, but I knew exactly where the sound had come from and who had made it and kept my eyes riveted on the three people standing below the altar.

Ellen's long veil and train successfully concealed any tremors which might otherwise have been visible and, after one astonished look round, Jeremy gripped her wrist and remained rigid as stone, his back squarely towards us.

Meanwhile, there had been murmurs and scuffles behind us, punctuated by a man's voice, slurred and protesting, and when I did turn I saw that five men were bunched up together, making a clumsy but concerted progress towards the door. One of them pulled it open and two others, each holding the arm of a third, went lurching out into the sunlight. Then the first man slammed the door behind them, letting the iron latch clang as it fell, advanced a few steps down the aisle and raised his hand in salute to the vicar, before he and his remaining companion returned to their seats.

Few ushers can have been called upon to play such an active role and the Rev. Donald Atkinson's experience was probably unique in the annals of Roakes parish history, so it was gratifying to find them all acquitting themselves with such admirable aplomb. After signalling to the organist and casting a sorrowful eye on those junior members of the choir who had succumbed to paroxysms of laughter, the vicar told us that we would now all join together in singing Psalm one hundred and thirteen, which, after an excusably ragged start, soon got into its stride, at which point I took a pen out of my bag and wrote a name on the hymn sheet, which I held up for Robin to read.

2

Toby had invited Robin and me to join the family party in the vestry, but as soon as he had been paired off with Stella Roxburgh and Irene had draped herself over Arnold's arm I whispered to Robin that he should follow on his own and slid off in the opposite direction, retracing my roundabout route to the back of the church.

One of our two remaining ushers left his seat to open the door for me, but most people were too busy gathering up their possessions and muttering to each other in decorous undertones to notice my departure.

The other two ushers were outside in the porch, facing each other on wooden benches and, in passing, I congratulated them on their efficient chucking out performance.

I did not stop to ask how the business had ended, which was probably a mistake, but I had another objective in view which at the time seemed more important.

As I had anticipated, Owen had already brought his limousine up to the gate and was relaxing behind the wheel with a cigarette. He threw it away when he saw me and strolled round to the nearside.

'Coming out now, are they?' he enquired.

'Not for another minute or two. They've gone to the vestry.'

'And there's still the photographs and all that lark, so plenty of time. Hope they get one of the old lady while they're at it. Looks a treat, doesn't she?' he asked, pointing with pride to the white satin streamers and rosettes which adorned the bonnet of his car.

'Yes, dreamy; but listen, Owen, there's something I want to ask you. It's about that hit-and-run accident you got mixed up in yesterday.'

'Oh yes?' he asked in a distant voice, clearly proclaiming that I had chosen an unsuitable moment to raise the topic. I agreed with him there, but I also knew that it might be my only chance, so I said:

'It's just a small thing, but I wanted to be sure that the story you told me over the telephone was exactly the same as you gave the police.'

'Any reason why it shouldn't have been?' he asked truculently.

'No, none at all, except that on the second time round, when you were talking to me, you might have left something out, either because you forgot, or because you were afraid it would worry me.'

Owen lit a fresh cigarette, cupping his hand round the flame to shield it from an imaginary breeze.

'Not that I know of. What's the game then? Did they come round to you, asking what I'd said?'

'No, this is just a personal enquiry.'

'You must be crackers! What could be personal about a thing like that?'

'To put it bluntly, it occurred to me that you could have noticed something about the accident which you didn't like to mention, in case it involved someone I knew. Those cars that passed you at the top of the hill, for instance? You didn't recognise one of them, did you?'

'No, I did not. I'd have spoken out like a shot if I had, wouldn't I? Catch me protecting someone who might have done a thing like that! You know the trouble with you, don't you? You've got crime on the brain. If some old woman tripped on the stairs and broke her neck, you'd have us all running round in circles while you tried to make out it was murder.'

'You could be right, but I'm not inventing complications this time. You see, I was talking to Mrs Lewis on the way here. The police want to see her and get a statement and she definitely gave me the impression that she had something important to tell them. I wondered if you had any idea what it could be?'

'No, I haven't and if that's all that's worrying you I should forget it. She was having you on, that's what. I mean, it stands to reason, doesn't it? Everything happened just like I said and she couldn't tell them any more than I could, if as much. You don't want to pay too much attention to that one. I know she's Miss Ellen's mother and I shouldn't speak against her, but if you ask me she's a real troublemaker. Say anything for devilment or to make herself the centre of attraction, wouldn't she? Watch it now, they're coming out, I do believe!' The bells were pealing again, the church door had opened and the photographers were moving up into position. Owen stubbed out his cigarette and I walked back to take my place in the latest fodder for the family album, only partially reassured by what I had heard. Owen's assessment of Irene's character and disposition might be dead on the mark, but he had overlooked one vital detail which undermined every assumption he had made.

3

'Come on!' Toby said, when the bride's procession had driven off, followed a few seconds later by the grey Rolls. 'You and Robin come with me.'

'How about Irene?'

'Simon's taking care of her. We may as well profit by it, so long as we're stuck with him.'

'Oh, very well, but you and Robin had better go ahead and I'll bring the Mercedes. Owing to one thing and another, I was the last to arrive and I'm parked several fields away.'

'All the better!'

'No, it isn't. You're supposed to be in line to receive us when we arrive.'

'Thank you very much,' Toby said grimly. 'I'd rather be dead.'

It was useless to argue with him when he was in this mood and we finally compromised with my driving him to the reception in our car, which had been directed to a very advantageous position by the village constable, while Robin gallantly trudged off to retrieve the Mercedes.

'Ellen didn't seem too badly put out by that ridiculous fraças,' I remarked as we took our place in the caterpillar of cars crawling back to the common.

'No, fortunately it would take more than that to ruffle those steely nerves. Who was responsible, do you know?'

'Desmond, of course. Who else?'

'Drunk?'

'I'm not sure about that. I saw him as I came in and he certainly looked ill, but it might have been pure hangover.'

'And how did those forceful young men dispose of him?'

'I didn't ask. It was stupid of me, I suppose, but I don't expect he put up much resistance once he was off stage. Desmond always prefers to conduct his private affairs in public and he probably made straight for the nearest pub, to air a few more grievances. Let's just hope he stays there until he passes out. Do you think we should stop off at the Bricklayers' and check up?'

'On the whole, I'd rather not. It would only lead to unpleasantness if we found him there, and we might become even more unnerved if he were not.'

'You prefer to remain in suspense?'

'Every time, and besides, if he should feel the urge to give us another little cameo performance at the reception I have implicit confidence in Robin to make short work of him. Unlike some, I never cease to be thankful that we have a policeman in the family.'

'And I suppose we might offer a vote of thanks to Jeremy for the fact that we don't have Desmond in the family?' I suggested, seeing the matter in this light for the first time and deriving some comfort from it.

'Oh, indeed! Although let us hope we shall find some more positive qualities to love and admire, as time goes by.'

'On the whole, I'd have preferred her to marry Simon, rather than Jeremy.'

'What a pity you didn't say so before,' Toby replied. 'Although personally I can't see that it would have made much difference to you and me, since they have both been cursed with the same parents.'

CHAPTER ELEVEN

1

I AWARDED Toby full marks for his foresight in refusing to take part in the reception line-up, for there was something ludicrous as well as inappropriate in this pompous prelude to a party for a hundred or so people, all of them relations or close friends, in a modest country garden. Unfortunately his absence had only served to increase the absurdity, for it had left Arnold Roxburgh on his own between the pink finery of Irene and the turquoise blue finery of Stella and, with his grey tail coat practically sweeping the grass, he looked like a little overfed, top-hatted pouter pigeon, preening himself on his two gorgeous mates.

We were among the last to arrive and when the M.C. had bellowed out his announcement of 'Mr and Mrs Crichton, er, beg pardon, Mr and Mrs Price', Ellen took it as a signal that the formalities were over and stepped out of line to be the first to greet us. After a nervous glance at his mother, Jeremy followed suit and the four of us formed into pairs and made our way towards the depths of the marquee.

'There's masses to eat,' Ellen said, taking my arm. 'That's one thing I did insist on, so mind you set a good example! There's nothing so brutal as expecting people to hang around for hours, drinking warm champagne on empty stomachs. And another brutal thing we mean to cut out is speeches. Simon has promised to keep his own down to four sentences and then Jeremy will thank everyone for coming and that'll be it.'

'It's not warm yet,' I assured her, having seized a glass from one of the battalion of waiters who were moving around with trays. 'In fact, it's beautifully cold.'

'Well, that can't last long, can it? Don't you find it stifling in here? Let's go out and take a turn in the garden.'

Some tables and chairs had been set out on the back lawn, where two more waiters were circulating with loaded trays and several of the guests had already found their way there. Ellen and I made the rounds, stopping at each table for a few gracious words and coming last of all to Jez, who was with a lively and colourful-looking group of younger guests, one of them dressed as a pantomime highwayman and another wearing a white sola topi. Caspar was seated on the grass nearby, a dish of nuts in front of him, and was busily transferring them, one by one and left and right, into two champagne glasses.

'I can't tell you why he does it,' Jez admitted. 'He's going through a cagey period at the moment. Perhaps he's laid bets with himself as to which glass will be filled up first, or it may be all part of the revolt against the accepted pattern of things. Yesterday he set himself to turning every book in the flat on its side. We were both quite worn out by the end of it. Of course he's a Gemini, you know, which makes everything even more obscure.'

'Like Desmond,' the highwayman remarked to no one in particular.

'Oh no, Desmond is Taurus, unmistakably so.'

Someone else said, 'I must say, Ellen, you took that fraças with marvellous cool, didn't you, love?'

'Naturally she would,' Jez said, tilting her head back and smiling up at Ellen, who was standing behind her. 'It's no more than we expect from our Virgos.'

'What's Jeremy's sign, by the way?' I asked.

'Oh Scorpio, of course. Wouldn't you know? Highly complicated characters, as a rule. To all but the Virgos,' Jez added with another lazy smile.

'I must go and find him,' Ellen said, smiling back. 'This is the last party ever where we'll be expected to stick together, so it would be a pity to waste it. Did you bring my address book, Jez?'

'Yes, it's indoors. I left it in the hall as we came by.'

'I was going to ask you about that scene in church,' I remarked as we re-traced our steps, 'but you both seemed to take it so calmly that I wondered afterwards if either of you had really understood what was going on.'

'We did and we didn't, if you know what I mean? I think we both thought we were going mad for a moment, but then it was over before we'd properly taken it in. Simon filled us in with the details when we got to the vestry. It's lucky Robert and Edward are such experienced rugby tacklers.'

'And how did they dispose of Desmond?'

'Oh, got one of the drivers to take him down to Stad-hampton. Apparently he came by train and was quite happy to go back the same way.'

I was both surprised and vaguely disturbed to hear this, for Desmond enjoyed nothing better than swooping down the M4 with one finger on the wheel pretending to be Jackie Stewart. However, there was always the possibility that his licence had been suspended again and in any case there was no point in shifting my worries on to Ellen, who then went on:

'Apparently there was no problem at all because he caved in at once when he found he was outnumbered and became as putty in their hands. Poor old Desmond! I blame myself, in a way.'

'You would, of course, but may one ask why?'

'Oh, because he wrote me a stupid letter, saying he was going to kill himself and God knows what, if I insisted on marrying Jeremy. I ought to have taken it more seriously, I suppose, but you remember how he was always threat-ening to kill himself or anybody else who happened to be annoying him. It didn't mean a thing. What mostly happens is that he has another drink or his agent sends him a play with a good part in it and all his persecution manias go flying out of the window. It's a shame really, because he's so lovely when things are going right for him, and such a drag when they're not.'

'Managements should be more alive to the problem.'

'You're so right, Tessa. Can't you use your influence? Oh look, there's poor Jeremy stuck with one of the Aunt Ednas! I must go and rescue him.'

2

Setting a good example, I bore down on the buffet table, which was L-shaped and ran half way across the back and down the whole of one length of the marquee. Opposite its longer side there were more sets of tables and chairs for the weaker vessels and, between these and directly under the highest point of the canopied roof, was a small, rectangular table, flanked at each end by a huge white urn of flowers. One half of this table was covered by ice buckets filled with champagne, the other being reserved for the yellow and white tiered wedding cake, which had been created by the pastry chef of Chey Bert.

There were several people hovering near the buffet table and I disposed of the more timid of these, with the help of the waiter in charge, by doling out helpings of cold roast duck and lobster mousse and by recommending them to move on down the line and pick up their own salad and wine. This left me standing midway between two more firmly entrenched groups, of whom the pair on my right, pressed up against the bar section, were two of Aunt Edna's male counterparts and had obviously been glued to the spot from the moment of their arrival. Giving them my full attention, I was rewarded by the following glimpse into other lives:

''Straordinary thing about that Croker boy! You see him?'

'No, can't say I did.'

'Unbelievable. Can't be more than fifteen, so Mary tells me. Grown a beard!'

'How 'straordinary!'

'Sprouting out all over him. Makes him look about forty.'

'Would do.'

'Extraordinary. When you think, I mean.'

This was not very fertile ground for eavesdropping, so I switched my attention to the left, where Irene was talking to that usher whom I now knew to be either Robert or Edward. Rather predictably, she was telling him all about her horrid experience on the drive from the airport and presumably the story was getting its third or fourth airing, since the grisly details had been hotted up to steaming pitch and her own part in it had developed into something positively saintly. Even so, it cannot have made compulsive listening, because Robert or Edward, who had been fidgeting quite overtly during its recital, took the first opportunity to cut in by saying: 'How absolutely rotten for you! What an awful shame! Oh, I say, your glass is empty! Do let me get you a refill?'

'How terribly sweet of you! Just a teeny one would be lovely. But not champagne, you know. It always makes me feel most frightfully ill.'

'I say, how rotten! What's it to be, then?'

'Just a teeny scotch and soda.'

'In a champagne glass?'

'It's the only kind they provide. I ask you!'

'Still, tastes just as good, I expect,' Robert or Edward said, picking up her glass and moving off with some speed. Irene called after him:

'Only a very, very weak one, remember, darling! I've got to say my piece to that cross-looking policeman later on and I must be awfully, awfully sober when I give him my statement.'

Fearful that she might now turn to me, for want of a more sympathetic audience, I too drifted away, carrying yet another piled-up plate. I had a vague idea of finding someone hungry enough to take it off me and, if that should be Phil, of introducing him to some of the younger elements, since it was unlikely that he had met any of them, or would have the initiative to take on this service for himself.

I did not find him, but eventually came across Alison, who was standing near the front opening and supporting herself against one of the posts. Her face was moist and streaked with orange powder and her whole bearing suggested a state of extreme mental and physical suffering.

'Whatever's the matter, Alison?'

'I'm in agony, if you want to know,' she muttered. 'These shoes are torture. I was a fool to put them on. As though any of this lot would notice or care what I was wearing!'

I looked down and was distressed to see that her feet had blown up like rubber tyres and that the rims of the high-heeled black kid shoes were biting into the swollen flesh.

'Why on earth don't you sit down? There are plenty of chairs over there.'

'I know, but I tried that and it was worse than ever. All I could think of was kicking them off and I knew if I did that I'd never get the blasted things on again. Besides, I'm watching out for Phil.'

'Have you lost him?'

'Looks suspiciously like it. Stalwart lad that he is, he nipped off home to fetch my everyday pair. Shouldn't have taken him more than five or six minutes, but he's been gone a good sight longer than that.'

'Oh, crumbs! So you think he might have . . . ?'

'Lost his nerve and chickened out? It's beginning to look like it. Not that he'd let me down deliberately, I know that, but then it's always a bit of a joke when women complain that their feet are killing them, so perhaps he didn't take it seriously.'

'And I can see it is serious,' I said. 'So here's what to do. Take this plate and go and sit at one of the tables. Then get your shoes off and relax until I get back.'

'What are you going to do? You won't find a pair of your own or Ellen's that I could squeeze into.'

'No, but I'll ring your house and find out what Phil's up to. If I can't persuade him to come back I'll go and fetch your shoes myself, or I'll rout out a pair of mules to see you through for the time being. Anyway, don't worry and don't prolong the agony. You'll turn gangrenous and have to have your legs amputated if you stand here much longer.'

I darted away, without waiting for her thanks, which I did not think would be forthcoming in any case.

A yew hedge separated the front lawn from the common and I took time out to sprint up to it and look over the top. There were at least forty cars parked on the other side, but, so far as I could see, not a single Mini among them. Nor was there any sign of Phil's approach along the track, although just for a second I was tricked into thinking I saw him leaning into one of the cars and talking to someone inside it. A pale-coloured jacket had caught my eye, but a moment later the man wearing it withdrew his head and stood upright, and I saw that it was not cream-coloured but pure white and that the wearer was one of the waiters. I could find no explanation for his being there, beyond a compulsive need to learn the result of the three o'clock at Doncaster from one of the chauffeurs, but there were more urgent problems requiring my attention and, having given the horizon a final scan, I turned my back on the scene and hurried into the house.

3

The hall felt cool and amazingly peaceful after the stuffy hubbub of the marquee and I was quite content to sit listening to the Ropers' number endlessly ringing away in my ear, long after I had abandoned hope of its being answered. The monotonous *brr brr* at the other end had a pleasantly soporific effect and I was only jolted out of a near torpor by the sight of Ellen's red leather address book.

It was lying on a chair just inside the front door and a pile of cards and letters had been pushed in between the cover and the top page. Jez had evidently deposited it there in one of her more haphazard moments, for several of the cards had slithered half way out and one or two of them had fallen on the floor.

I put the receiver back, walked over to the chair, replaced all the correspondence inside the book and took it up to Ellen's room. I was not indifferent to Alison's sufferings, but, since a minimum of five minutes would have to elapse before I should know whether Phil had not answered the telephone because he felt disinclined to, or because he had already started on the return journey, it was a question of putting the interval to some useful account.

Ellen's overnight bag was packed and ready, but had been left open for last-minute additions and, having placed the address book on top, I used up another two minutes on repairs to my face before slowly descending to the hall again. Good timing too, for as I reached the front door I saw Phil walking up the garden path, carrying a green and white plastic bag from the supermarket.

'You've certainly taken your time,' I remarked, and he first flushed and scowled at me as though I had accused him of rape and incest and then rapidly climbed down by saying:

'I'm awfully sorry. It wasn't my fault.'

'Well, don't bother to apologise to me. Save it for your mother. She's on the point of explosion.'

'Yes, I expect I'll get a rocket,' he said sulkily, 'but how can I help it if she insists on wearing shoes she's had in her wardrobe for about ten years? I offered to chip in for a new pair, but she wouldn't let me. And it took ages to find her other black ones. She said they were in the hall cupboard but they weren't. I had to go looking all through her bedroom and then, just as I was leaving, the telephone rang, so I had to go back indoors and answer it and by the time I got there whoever it was had rung off.'

Rather to my embarrassment, all this was related on a rising note of self-pity and ended with Phil's rubbing his eye, as though some grit had lodged in it. It made me understand why Alison worried herself to death about his being so unhappy, but I could not help wondering whether her ceaseless jollying and nagging had not contributed, even more than Ellen's faithlessness, to making him so spineless and whether attendance at Reading University, enabling him to spend every weekend with his old Mum, had been such a sound idea, after all.

'Never mind, you're here now, which is all that matters. So do come on, then,' I added impatiently as he still lingered, mulishly looking back over his shoulder. 'We don't want to waste any more time.'

'I was wondering where that waiter had got to,' he mumbled.

'Back to his post, presumably. Do hurry up!'

'There's something funny about him, if you ask me,' Phil said, reluctantly falling into step and moving forward at last. 'He keeps bobbing up and then disappearing again.'

'Oh really? Well, that's his business, I suppose.'

'Well, I think he's up to something, in case you're interested.'

I was not at all interested, but, thinking it might help Phil to forget his own troubles, I made enquiring noises.

'He was out there on the common when I started off to fetch Mum's shoes, and I saw him getting into one of the cars. When I came back just now, there he was on the common.'

'Well, I never!'

'And he had a moustache.'

'Probably the Croker boy up to his tricks. No, no, that was only a joke,' I added hastily as Phil stopped in his tracks again. 'What I meant to say was: Why shouldn't he have a moustache? He's probably Italian.'

'No, you don't understand. He didn't have a moustache the first time I saw him and the second time he did. I think you're right about its being someone playing a trick. I don't believe he's a waiter at all.'

We had come to within a few paces of the marquee by this time and the hum of talk and laughter from the dim interior had risen to a sustained roar.

'Either that,' I said loudly, 'or what you saw were two separate waiters. Probably one of them owns a car and they all take it in turns to nip out there for a smoke. Look, there's your mother, over on the right. She's looking pretty desperate, so you'd better run along and put her out of her misery.'

'Okay, okay,' Phil said, with a return to the surly manner. 'Only don't blame me if you get back to the house this evening and find all the silver's been pinched.'

4

The operation had been completed only in the nick of time, for it was now two-fifteen and I knew that the toasts and cake-cutting ceremony were scheduled to start at two-thirty, Ellen and Jeremy having planned to leave as soon as they were over, so as to be on the road by three o'clock.

In preparation for this climax, several waiters were already making a tour of the marquee refilling champagne glasses, while another was engaged in opening bottles in the bucket on the central table. I gave particular attention to each of them and was rewarded with the useless information that two had moustaches, while the rest did not. There remained one more, still at his post behind the buffet table, also clean-shaven, and I went up to him, meaning to ask if the full roster was present and correct. However, before I could speak he raised his eyebrows at me in a despairing fashion and pointed along the table to his right. This was the spot where Irene had been giving her all to Robert or Edward and it was now occupied by Caspar, his chin just level with the table's edge and an expression of fierce concentration on his pallid face. There were half a dozen plates containing the remainders of assorted canapes within reach of his frail but purposeful little hands and he was using them to brush up for his next I.Q. test, setting each square morsel out on the tablecloth and matching it up with its fellows. He had reached the stage where all the caviar was in one straight row at the top and all the smoked salmon, like the thin red line gallantly opposing the Zulus, just below it. He was currently at work on the prawns, which was an exciting stage in the game for it looked as though they might end by forming the longest line of all, though clearly the anchovy and egg would be close runners-up.

I found myself becoming quite engrossed by the exercise but had my attention abruptly wrenched away by Simon coming up from the rear and giving me a brisk pat on the shoulder.

'I have to start my speech in a minute. Got any professional tips?'

'Just remember to breathe,' I advised him. 'Keep your voice up and take it slowly. Anyway, I was given to understand that your part had been cut to a couple of rhubarbs?'

'Those were my instructions, but I regard them as flexible. I don't want to disappoint my audience and if I cut it too short it will all be over before they realise I've begun. I thought that once I'd got their attention with a joke or two, I'd raise my glass to the young couple, wish them long life and happiness and bid them go forward together, hand in hand, to create a better moral climate in this great country of ours. Or words to that effect. How does it strike you?'

'I should think it would do very nicely.'

'Right, then I rely on you to lead off with the "Hear hears" and "Bravos".'

'There is something I should perhaps do for you before that, Simon. Part of your audience is still out in the garden. Shouldn't I go and round them up?'

'Good thinking! I should appreciate it enormously. And I've met your husband, by the way. Fine figure of a man. It has given me second thoughts about inviting you to dinner this evening.'

Jez was still holding court in the garden, the number of people surrounding her having more than doubled. Several extra tables had been brought up and placed beside hers and the party now included Robert or Edward, as well as the two elder bridesmaids, but unfortunately not Phil. She had a knack of forming a party within a party wherever she went and I knew that it would only be necessary for me to invite her to accompany me into the marquee for all the rest to follow, like a flock of flamingos taking off in the sunset.

'You are wanted inside,' I told her. 'The climax is approaching and Caspar needs a wipe down.'

Her face fell and she stood up with most untypical haste.

'Is he all right? Has anything happened to him?' she asked, displaying a degree of maternal solicitude I had not known her to possess.

'Of course he's all right. Why shouldn't he be?'

'I don't know, Tess. It's just that I felt the most sinister vibrations when you said that. It's strange because normally yours are very harmonious.'

'Not necessarily when I've been drinking champagne on a hot afternoon, though.'

Despite her dedication to her calling, Jez always took teasing with the utmost good humour and she smiled at once and said,

'Too right. Let us weave our halting way inside and see what the little man is up to.'

The action had moved forward during this three-minute interval and all glasses were now filled and at the ready. Everyone, including Alison, was standing and eight of the nine principals had moved into position round two sides of the central table. Simon was at the top and narrower end, nearest to his audience, and next to him Jeremy who had Ellen on his other side. At right angles to them, Irene, swaying a little, was at the head of the longer line, looking flushed and about ten years older than at the start of the festivities. Her make-up had wilted under the onslaught of heat and fatigue, not to mention a steady intake of scotch and, as though aware of the damage, she had concealed the upper half of her face behind enormous sun glasses.

Arnold stood just below her, beaming and waving his pale, pudgy hand at anyone who caught his eye, with Stella looming beside him as cool, stern and immaculate as ever. Next came Robin and after him Toby who signalled to me, in a somewhat despairing way, to come over and protect his other flank. I did so, placing myself round the corner at the foot of the table, behind the only unclaimed glass and directly facing the three at the top.

Caspar had edged himself as close as possible to this scene and was observing it with an inscrutable expression which barely quivered when Jez scooped him up under her arm and sauntered back into the crowd of onlookers. All was now hushed and expectant and Simon held up his hand like a policeman on point duty, then winked at me and began:

'Ladies and gentlemen, may I crave your attention, please?'

Anyone who knew Irene might, I dare say, have fore-seen what occurred next, yet I guessed that even Toby was taken aback. Every eye was on Simon, now filling his lungs for the second time and, with exact and perfect timing, she piped up:

'Before you begin, I wonder if someone would be kind enough to find me a chair?'

There was a moment of stupefied blankness, the first sign of movement coming from the waiters, now ranged together at the back of the marquee by the buffet table and appearing considerably more numerous than had been the case when they were all flitting around as indi-viduals. Two of them had now detached themselves and were approaching but, apart from this and from assum-ing alert and obliging expressions, there was nothing they could do to alleviate the situation, being separated from all the available chairs by a closely packed throng of guests. In the meantime, though, there had been a rustle of activity among this faction too and people were edging aside and pushing into each other to make way for

Phil, coming through from the back and audibly cheered on by his mother with a chair held high above his head.

'I am so terribly sorry to be such a bother,' Irene said, speaking now with vastly overdone humility, 'but I'm not feeling frightfully well and it would be so awful if I were to spoil things for everybody by fainting. Do please forgive me for making such a fuss, but it's so dreadfully hot in here, isn't it?'

There followed a rather ludicrous skirmish, in which Phil, having reached the table, showed every indication of intending to pass the chair over the top of it, realising a second or two later than the rest of us that in doing so he was liable to wreck the top tier of the wedding cake, and remaining fixed like a statue, while the chair wobbled in his grasp. Simon leapt into the breach, reaching up to steady the chair with one hand, while with the other he gestured to Phil to pass it round behind him to the waiter who stood with outstretched hands to receive it at the other end. This of course meant putting the urn of flowers at risk and, although everyone in his passage backed away to allow Phil a clear space, he still managed to catch a chair leg in the trailing stems of an orchid and then, scarlet in the face with embarrassment, to tug it away too sharply so that for a breathless moment we all watched horrified as the whole magnificent edifice swayed gently back and forth on its base.

Ellen gave a slight scream, which could have stemmed from either laughter or exasperation; Simon, moving like a snake, somehow got both hands on the urn to steady it, and Phil made the final plunge through to safety, banging the chair down beside Irene with such force that he lost his balance and all but collapsed on to it himself. If she had sat up all night planning the details, which she may have done for all I know, she could not have hit upon a neater way of disrupting the party and causing acute embarrassment to all present.

Naturally order was not immediately restored and Irene even managed to create a little extra confusion by sinking down on the chair in an exhausted fashion and then making a big production number over being unable to find her bag, although she could scarcely have seen it through the black glasses if it had been propped up on the table in front of her.

A little more scuffling around ensued before the bag was restored to her, whereupon she smiled apologetically in the direction of Simon, at the same time opening it and fishing out a tiny silver box. Turning his back on her, Simon raised his glass and addressed the audience: 'Ladies and gentlemen!' he said in a quiet, almost conversational tone, 'I give you the bride and bridegroom! May they always enjoy happiness and peace!' he added, laying a slight emphasis on the last word.

A hundred glasses were raised and, as the murmur of a hundred voices repeating the toast died away, Irene shot her last bolt. She tilted her glass, took a deep and thirsty draught, then, gasping and spluttering, made a move to set it down on the table, misjudging the distance, so that it tipped over and fell on to the ground. Clutching her stomach, she let out a piercing scream:

'My God, someone's mixed champagne in my . . .'

She began to choke and a moment later swayed forward, before toppling sideways on to the grass.

5

Robin was the first to reach her, dropping on to his knees and simultaneously pushing the chair aside to provide more space. The glass had rolled underneath and he instinctively stretched out his hand towards it, but there were now not less than five pairs of feet curvetting around and one of them stepped on the glass and crushed it into the ground, although he had no way of telling whether this had been done deliberately, still less of identifying the owner of the foot in question. On reflection, he was inclined to rule out Arnold, since his memory of the incident remained clear enough to suggest that it had belonged to a much larger man.

'Stand back everyone, please!' he called, getting up and doing so himself. 'I think she's fainted and we need all the air we can get. Is one of you a doctor, by any chance?' he went on, in a slight variation of the time honoured question.

A small, pale and bespectacled man pushed his way through from the back and advanced to the table. He was dressed like all the others in grey morning coat, but Robin had no need to ask for credentials, for his name was Dr Macintosh and he practised in Stadhampton. He had been in regular attendance on the Crichton household ever since they moved to Roakes and, being almost as confirmed a hypochondriac as Toby, it would have been hard for an onlooker to guess, during one of their frequent consultations, which one of them was treating the other.

'I haven't got my bag of tricks with me,' he explained. 'But if she's fainted the best thing would be to move her out to the garden.'

Robin shook his head very slightly and, interpreting this almost imperceptible movement correctly, Dr Macintosh cocked an eye at him and then moved rapidly round to the other side of the table, passing behind Ellen and giving her shoulder a pat as he went by. She was the only one of us who had not moved from her place and she neither acknowledged Dr Macintosh's comforting little gesture, nor turned her head as he crouched down beside Irene, and this unusual reaction, combined with a curious stiffness in her attitude, prompted me to observe her more intently. She was staring straight ahead of her, with a wary, puzzled expression on her face and as I watched she stretched out her hand, whipped up one of the three glasses on her end of the table and emptied the contents on to the ground.

Meanwhile a muttered exchange had passed between Robin and the doctor, at the end of which Robin detached himself and came down the table to speak to Toby and me.

'I'm going to telephone for an ambulance and I think the best thing, Toby, would be to try and get everyone to leave as soon as possible.'

'Is it serious?' I asked.

'She's in a bad way, I'm afraid. Looks like a heart attack, but there's no need to go into details. Just say she's been taken ill, but whatever happens get it through to them that the party's over.'

'In that case, why not stay here and help Toby hustle them out and let me do the telephoning?'

'Because I've another job for you, Tess. Come on, and I'll explain as we go.'

I hurried after him, but as soon as we were outside the marquee he stood still and said:

'Listen, I've only dragged you out here to make certain we aren't overheard, and I want you to go straight back in again and grab Ellen and Jeremy. Push them out as unobtrusively as you can and see they get changed as fast as possible. And remind Simon to have their car at the gate with the keys inside. He was going to do that anyway, but it might slip his mind with all this bother going on.'

'What's the hurry?' I asked. 'Wouldn't it be more sensible for them to leave quietly, when the crowd has thinned out?'

'No, it wouldn't. To put it mildly, it's going to be unpleasant for them if they're still here when the ambulance arrives. Not a particularly auspicious start to married life and the less they get mixed up in it the fewer disagreeable memories they'll be stuck with.'

He had started to walk away, but I caught up with him, saying,

'I've a feeling there's more to it than that. Are you hinting that it wasn't a straightforward heart attack, after all?'

Reluctantly stopping again, he replied:

'Honestly, Tess, there's no time to go into it now, but you must see that whether she died from natural causes or not is beside the point at the moment. Macintosh never clapped eyes on her, in the medical sense, until a few moments ago. He can't possibly sign a certificate in the circumstances. All I want is to ensure that Ellen and Jeremy are far away when the questions start. Just tell her that her mother's had a heart attack, not necessarily fatal, and that we'll keep her informed by cable.'

6

People had been walking past us in increasing numbers during this interlude and I saw why as soon as I re-entered the marquee. Stella had taken over Toby's function of herding the guests to their cars and was making a much more competent job of it than he would have done. There was a combination of poise and imperiousness in her manner, which conveyed that all was for the best in the best of all possible weddings, while at the same time effectively quelling any inclination to remain a single moment longer to enjoy it.

Moreover, she had already set some of my own wheels in motion and broke off the gracious handshakes to inform me in an aside that Ellen and Jeremy had left by the back entrance. Simon had his brother in charge and Ellen was waiting for me in her room.

It was doubtless also thanks to her efficiency that a screen had been brought over from the house and was now being placed around Dr Macintosh and his patient. It was one which Ellen and I had decorated with a montage of animal pictures from colour magazines during her measles convalescence, and the pandas and Shetland ponies and kittens peeping out of baskets certainly looked rather incongruous but, since for the past four hours we all seemed to have been treading the razor's edge between tragedy and farce, I regarded this as quite an appropriate *coup de grâce.*

I could hear Simon's high-pitched voice burbling away as I arrived on the upstairs landing, and he stuck his head round the door in answer to my knock.

'Managing all right?' I enquired.

'A good question! Basically, the situation could be described as fluid. However, one presses on.'

'Anything I can do to help?'

'No, thanks ever so much. Normally, one would cry for a double scotch as the answer to this crisis, but our recent experience rather seems to rule that out. However, be of good cheer and we shall all win through.'

I passed on Robin's reminder about the car and proceeded to Ellen's room.

She had removed her veil and head-dress, but had made no further attempt to change and was sitting on her bed, pale and rigid as a pillar of salt.

'What's the matter?' I asked. 'Can't you get your dress undone? Come on! Stand up and I'll do it for you.'

'She's dead, isn't she, Tessa?'

'Oh, goodness, no,' I replied with barely a falter. 'Whatever gave you that idea? It's only a little heart attack and she'll probably be all right in a day or two. She'll have to go to hospital, though, and Robin thinks you and Jeremy should aim to leave before the ambulance arrives.'

'What's the point of sending for an ambulance when she's dead? You know jolly well she's dead, so why pretend?'

'All right, then, I'll admit her condition is said to be serious, but even so you can't spend the rest of your life in a wedding dress. Come on, now! Jeremy's almost ready to leave.'

'I'm not sure that I want to go, though. I've a feeling that I ought to stay here.'

She spoke in a flat, almost childlike voice which foxed me completely and this, on top of all the trials that had gone before, tempted me to throw in the sponge. However,

I struggled to keep my patience for she was obviously in a state of mild shock, although it was hard to see why. It was less than twenty-four hours since she had re-met her mother, after a separation of fifteen years and I had certainly not detected any signs of affection on either side when communications were resumed. All the same, Ellen was devoid of affection and it was even less credible that she could be putting on an act. I was left with the conclusion that the passive rebellion arose from a reluctance to go away with Jeremy, rather than from grief on Irene's account and in a strange roundabout way this was true, although the full explanation still lay some way ahead.

'What do you want to do, then?' I asked, striving to sound as though this were the most normal conversation in the world. 'Stay here until we get some news of Irene and perhaps take the night ferry instead? Or spend the night here and see how you feel about things in the morning? If so, I expect Jeremy will understand and not mind too much, but you'd better decide, so that I know what to tell him. We can't just sit here and let it rip.'

'What I'd really like to do,' Ellen said, quietly tossing another little bombshell into my lap, 'if you wouldn't mind awfully arranging it for me, is to talk to Robin.'

'Oh really? Well, I don't see why not. Very sound idea, in fact; but I tell you what: why not get the finery off and step into a dressing gown? You'll be much more comfortable. Then I'll go and find him.'

'Okay,' she agreed and to my great relief stood up at last, raising her hands behind her head to start on the back fastenings.

'Perhaps he won't be able to come, though,' she added as I attacked the lower hooks for her. 'Then what'll I do?'

'No reason why he shouldn't. Perhaps not right away, but very soon, I expect. On the other hand, if you don't feel like waiting, why don't I take a message to him and bring back the answer?'

'Well yes, I suppose that might do,' she replied, stepping out of the dress which she left in a heap on the floor, while she wrapped herself in the white candlewick robe. She sounded more alive and composed now, as though a decision had been taken and some of the burden eased.

'Right, so what am I to ask him?'

'Two things. First of all, was Irene murdered?' Considering Robin's advice and instructions on how to handle the situation, I did not envisage any particularly fervent congratulations when I passed on this simple question and, in hopes of toning it down a little, I said: 'I'm perfectly certain such an idea hasn't entered his head and I can't imagine where you got it from. Admittedly, she had a certain faculty for rubbing people up the wrong way, but that didn't make her immune to all the usual physical weaknesses. In fact, Robin says that everything points to its being a heart attack. And why not? She'd had a particularly gruelling forty-eight hours and it will probably turn out that she had a weak heart, anyway.'

'The second thing I want you to ask him,' Ellen said, having waited with the utmost civility for me to finish speaking and then continuing as though I had not done so at all, 'is whether the poison, or whatever it was that killed her, was in the drink. That's the really important bit.'

I waited for her to expand on this but she was sitting on the bed again, regarding me with an impassive expression. evidently under the impression that further explanation would be superfluous.

'Oh, all right, if you insist, but don't be surprised if he takes the attitude that you're being thoroughly childish. I mean, just supposing for the sake of argument that she died from unnatural causes and, if she is dead, I suppose no one could say categorically at this point that it wasn't so, how in the world could you expect Robin or anyone else to tell you what caused it? All that kind of thing has to be decided by pathologists and so on.'

This line of reasoning appeared to impress her more than any I had tried before and she nodded approvingly, as though relieved to hear me talking sense at last.

'Yes, I hadn't thought of that; so tell me, Tessa, how long does all that usually take?'

Before I could answer we were interrupted by a sharp rap on the door, which was just a trifle too much for my frayed nerves to take in their stride, and it was Ellen who called out:

'Yes? Who is it?'

'Me. Simon. Just to let you know that we're all set and I'll be revving up the engine in a couple of mins.'

Bouncing back to mobility again, I flung myself at the door and caught up with him as he reached the staircase. Then, having made sure the spare-room door was closed, I said:

'Hold it, will you, Simon? We need another ten or fifteen minutes minimum.'

'Oh really? Well, just as you say, old lady, but I understood the idea was to move fast? Weren't they supposed to make a dash for it?'

'Yes, but we've run into a snag. Can't explain now, but I'm working on it. Tell Jeremy she can't find her shoes, any old thing that comes into your head, but for God's sake see there's no panic. We're in enough trouble already.'

I retreated to Ellen's room before he could give utterance to even one of the questions I could see bursting up in him, and she said, once more as though there had been no interruption,

'How long would all that take, then, Tessa?'

'Post mortem and analysts' reports and so on? It varies, I believe, but not less than twenty-four hours. It might be longer in this case because all her previous medical history is tucked away in some filing cabinet in Winnipeg. So, you see, Robin is as much in the dark as the rest of us and there'd be no point in hanging around on that account. You can telephone me every evening from France and I promise faithfully to let you know the results the minute we hear them. Does that make you feel any better?'

As I finished speaking I heard a bell clanging far away in the distance, but growing louder every instant and a dismal reminder, had I needed one, of how badly I had mismanaged Robin's scheme to get Ellen and Jeremy off the premises before this distressing event occurred. I walked over to the window and looked out across the common, where, apart from Jeremy's red sports number, only two cars now remained, and watched the white ambulance come into view and then trundle along the track towards us. When I turned round I saw that Ellen had gone tense again and was huddled into the white robe as though chilled to the bone, so I said,

'I'm so sorry, darling. It would be stupid to pretend that your wedding has been a very happy occasion and I do understand how you feel.'

'No, you don't,' she replied flatly. 'You couldn't possibly understand, because what I feel is that it should have been Jeremy they were carting away in that thing and perhaps next time it will be.'

'Are you mad? What possible reason can you have for saying such a thing?'

'The best. That is, if she was poisoned and if the poison was in her glass, as I feel it must have been.'

'Could you explain, perhaps?'

'Well, you see, Tess, there was a bit of a mix-up.'

'You could describe it like that, I suppose.'

'And poor old Irene got the wrong glass. I suppose she was a bit pie-eyed, for a start, and obviously she couldn't see much through those glasses. Anyway, that's what must have happened and I can't pretend to be truly sorry because, if she hadn't snapped it up, the chances are that I should now be a widow.'

'How did you work all that out?'

'It didn't take genius. You see, when Simon gave the toast, Jeremy and I were the only two who didn't pick up our glasses, right?'

'I'm with you, so far.'

'Everyone else did, including Irene, and the very next thing that happened was that she keeled over and passed out. You remember that all right?'

'Yes, clearly.'

'So everyone started jumping about and crowding round her. Everyone except me, that is.'

'And why not you?'

'Because, God forgive me, I thought it was just one more little gimmick to draw attention to herself. I thought she so hated anyone else having the limelight that she'd even go to those lengths to grab it back. I was so furious that I couldn't even bring myself to look at her, and do you know what I did instead?'

'No.'

'I thought to myself that while we were waiting for the latest little drama to play itself out, I'd drink a private toast all to myself: "Here's to my long lost unlamented mother and may she never cross my path again!" That's what I said to myself and I picked up my glass to drink to it. Only I don't think it was my glass, actually. We'd all shifted around a bit by then and I'm almost sure it was the one which had been nearest to Jeremy. Naturally that didn't bother me because they all had champagne in them, except that . . .'

'This one didn't?'

'You've caught on at last, have you? No, this one had whisky in it. I could tell by the smell, without even tasting it. So it must have been poured out for Irene and either the waiter made a mistake, or else the glasses got moved around when Phil brought the chair over. That part doesn't matter. The important thing is that someone must have meant to poison Jeremy. Irene yelled out something about having champagne in her whisky, but it wasn't that at all. Someone had put poison in Jeremy's champagne, and how am I to know they won't try again?'

PART TWO

CHAPTER ONE

The Times, Monday, 28th May.

Mr J. Roxburgh and
Miss E.S.R. Crichton.

The marriage between Mr Jeremy Roxburgh, elder son of Mr and Mrs Arnold Roxburgh and Miss Ellen Crichton, daughter of Mr Toby Crichton and the late Mrs O.E. Lewis, took place at St Mary's Parish Church, Roakes, Oxfordshire, on Saturday, 26th May. The bride was given in marriage by her father and Mr Simon Roxburgh, brother of the bridegroom, was best man. The honeymoon will be spent motoring in France and Italy.

Lewis, Irene Margaret. On 26th May of a heart attack while holidaying in England. Funeral private. Memorial service in Winnipeg to be announced later.

Both these proclamations were the work of Stella Roxburgh, who presumably operated on the principle that anything printed in *The Times* was bound to come true, although, in fact, by the time they appeared it had been established beyond doubt that Irene had died of paraquat poisoning and Ellen and Jeremy were still firmly entrenched on their own side of the Channel, having journeyed no further than London and intending, so far as anyone could tell, to spend their honeymoon in Jeremy's flat in Hans Crescent.

'Wouldn't you have thought,' Robin asked me, as we drove back to London ourselves on Monday morning, 'if she genuinely believes someone is out to murder Jeremy, that her instinct would be to get him to the Continent and out of harm's way and to stay there until all this is cleared up?'

'Not necessarily. She may feel he is less vulnerable at the flat than trotting around foreign hotels, possibly with the murderer on their trail. There was no secret about their route, so it wouldn't be too hard for him to bob up with another dose of paraquat along the way.'

We were approaching the airport intersection of the M4 by this time and a stream of traffic was racing up to join us. Robin switched over to the outside lane to give them a clear field and it was several minutes before he spoke again. Then he said:

'Keeping an eye on Jeremy could have two interpretations.'

'Yes, I know.'

'And, on the face of it, don't you find her behaviour more consistent with the second?'

'Meaning that her motive is not to protect him, but herself?'

'Right.'

'But that implies that it was untrue that she picked up his glass instead of her own and found it contained whisky. I've had the feeling all along that she was holding something back, but why lie about a thing like that? If it was really her own glass and not his that Irene drank from, why not have said so?'

'Presumably because if the poison was intended for herself the only person who is likely to have put it there is Jeremy. If you recall the scene you'll remember that he was standing between Ellen and his brother, but Irene was round the corner, so to speak; and, placed like that, it would have been understandable if Irene had mistaken Ellen's glass for her own. On the other hand, Jeremy's would have been several inches away and to pick it up would have necessitated stretching her arm across the table. It would have been such an awkward movement that I'm sure we should have noticed.'

'Ellen's story is that all three glasses got shifted around during the fuss of Phil bringing the chair over.'

'Nevertheless, I can't see why Jeremy's glass should have been moved. Irene's perhaps, to save it from being knocked off the table, but surely Jeremy's would only have been shifted further forward, away from the edge, not down towards Irene's corner?'

'Are you seriously suggesting that Jeremy could have set out to murder Ellen within two hours of marrying her? She's not an heiress, you know. The rich boot is on the other foot.'

'I'm not suggesting anything; only that there's a remote possibility that she may have taken it into account.'

'Then why cover up? If she suspects him to be capable of such a monstrous thing, why not leave him and have the marriage annulled?'

'Because if by any chance he were guilty he would understand her reasons for doing that and she would be a bigger danger to him than she is already; therefore to be silenced at all costs.'

'But this is terrible, Robin! Why haven't you told me before? How can she be left alone with him in the flat, if her life is in danger?'

'I don't imagine it is. As I see it, there is only an even chance that the poison was in the drink, which in turn gives the faint chance that it was intended for Ellen and not Irene. There remains the question of who put it there. Naturally, she would be reluctant to include Jeremy among her suspects, but there may be just enough doubt in her mind to make her even more reluctant to go abroad with him, just the two of them, driving along lonely mountainous roads, to name only one of the possible hazards. The sensible course would be to stay in London until there is evidence to prove Jeremy innocent.'

'But could one really suspect someone one was in love with of being so vile?'

'Such things have been known, haven't they? And Ellen has her feet on the ground. She only met Jeremy a few months ago and there must be vast chunks of his past which are unknown to her, not to mention facets of his character. And you've told me yourself you weren't sure just how overboard she actually was.'

'I know, Robin, but even so! Even if it's not a desperate, consuming passion, she must be fond of him, or she would never have married him. The money part wouldn't enter into it, whatever some people may say.'

'All the same, she can't altogether ignore the fact that, if the poison was intended for her, Jeremy was among the very few who had an opportunity to slip it to her.'

'Though presumably the same thing applies if it was intended for Irene?'

'No, that would be quite different. In Irene's case the poison could equally well have been in her pills, which completely knocks out the idea that someone within range of her was necessarily responsible. She could have been carrying poisoned pills around with her for weeks. The police carted away stacks of bottles and phials which they found in her luggage and, according to Alison, she was dosing herself with some drug or other every few hours. She claimed that her nerves were all to pieces because of the road accident, but I should put her down as one who made a regular habit of that sort of thing and, if that was the method, the murderer only needed to bide his time. He could have been thousands of miles away when she actually died.'

'Well, that's a cheering thought. So perhaps it was Osgood, after all? Unfortunately, she did yell out that someone had mixed champagne with her whisky, so it must have had a pretty funny taste.'

'Well, so it would to someone who was expecting one and got the other. I don't suppose she was choosing her words very carefully.'

'And how long will it be before they know?'

'Know what?'

'Whether it was the pills or the drink that did it?'

'Short of a confession, never, I imagine,' Robin said, pulling over to the right-hand lane once more, as the Cromwell Road spread out ahead of us in all its glory. 'In the first place, they were swallowed simultaneously and, as you know, the glass fell on the ground and was smashed almost to a powder before anyone realised it was serious. If it had only happened indoors, there might have been a patch of carpet to be analysed, remains of the glass too, but no chance of that on well-watered turf, where it had been stamped on and crushed into the ground by half a dozen hefty feet.'

This mention of turf reminded me of something else and I said:

'But, Robin, isn't paraquat used as a weed killer?'

'In diluted form, yes.'

'So even if there'd only been dregs left in Irene's glass, wouldn't it have shown up in the form of dead blades of grass on that spot?'

'Yes, but unfortunately that wouldn't have been conclusive. Parkes was interrogated on the point and he keeps a supply of the stuff in his tool shed, in its diluted form, such as anyone can buy over the counter. Of course he dilutes it still further by mixing it in about twenty parts of water and he uses a special watering can with a long spout. The trouble is that he scatters the stuff around all over the place, even on the lawn, if he sees a plantain or daisy rearing its ugly head, specially at this time of year when weeds are at their most prolific. He'd been working flat out, up to late on Friday evening when the marquee went up, to get the garden looking spick and span, and he made numerous journeys across the lawn carrying that particular can and probably not worrying too much if it dribbled some out as he went. So a tiny tuft of dead grass wouldn't really prove anything.'

'And it begins to look as though Ellen may have a good long wait before her honeymoon can begin.'

'Oh, it's early days yet and a lot may come to light in the next twenty-four hours. Osgood is supposed to be arriving tonight and he may have something to contribute. Do you want to go straight home, or shall I drop you somewhere?'

'Anywhere round here would do, if you can find a place to stop.'

'Going for a tour round Harrods?'

'Not a serious one. Just in by the front door and out by the back.'

'Oh, I see. Well, give whoever it is my love, and do mind how you go!'

Taking this warning literally, I virtuously trotted up the road to a pedestrian crossing, before darting across to the other side, and then spent several minutes in contemplation of a waxen female in a sheepskin coat, seated on a shooting stick, with a stuffed poodle and a vase of plastic flowers at her feet, as I considered how best to handle the next encounter.

CHAPTER TWO

THE front door was off the latch and I pushed it open with one hand, rang the bell with the other and marched inside.

'Yes, we mostly do leave it unfastened nowadays,' Jez explained, when I had tracked her down in the kitchen, where all her charts and reference books were spread out on the table. 'Caspar likes to answer the bell himself, you see, and he can't reach the handle. Ellen was always so patient about it, but I get madly bored trudging into the hall to do half the job for him, and then disappearing again while he finishes it off. Would you like some coffee?'

'Yes, please. Where's Caspar now?'

'Asleep, so you may speak freely. Did you come to see me, or had you forgotten that Ellen had moved out?'

Having based my strategy on the assumption that Jez was both too lazy and too direct to give a crooked answer to a straight question, I did not hesitate to reply:

'I am here to ask whether, in your considered opinion, Ellen suspects Jeremy of having attempted to murder her?'

'No.'

'Then how do you account for the current state of affairs?'

'Wait until I've ground the coffee,' Jez replied as placidly as though we were discussing the weather, 'and you shall have my interpretation, but this thing makes a noise like a road drill.'

I waited while she flipped switches and pressed buttons and the scream of the coffee grinder filled the room. Then she tipped the contents into a paper cone, saying gravely;

'Ellen would never believe that Jeremy could act in any way harmfully towards her. I am not sure that she was so dead set on marrying him, at any rate not so soon. I think she may have got steamrollered into that. His mother wasn't taking no for an answer and Jeremy, having made his one tiny bid for freedom, which turned out so disastrously, had lost the will to stand up to her. I think it's this feeling of being jostled along by all the family pressures which has tended to make Ellen a bit jumpy and withdrawn these days, not quite her usual serene self; but that's not to say that she doesn't trust Jeremy. She feels very strongly that they are right for each other and if the only way to get him was to marry him, then wedding bells it had to be.'

'An attitude to which you have contributed your share?'

'Well, that's beside the point, isn't it?' Jez said mildly, as she handed me my coffee. 'I happen to believe they are right for each other too, but it makes no difference where she got the idea from in the first place. You asked me if it was conceivable that she could suspect Jeremy of trying to murder her and I've given you your answer.'

'Which does nothing to explain why they're now skulking in Hans Place, instead of racing round France and Italy.'

'I imagine the reason is that there would be no pleasure in it. The shadow is there all right, only it hangs over and not between them. They want to stick around until it's been shooed away, in other words until it's established that someone set out to kill the dreadful mother and not one of them. They don't seem terribly optimistic about it either, which is rather a surprise. Personally, I regard it as a safe bet. The only mystery is how she managed to exist for so long before somebody decided to rid the world.'

'In that case, wouldn't it be safer for them to go, rather than stay? Since they don't suspect each other, they ought to be able to protect each other, even if the murderer were to follow them.'

'You might think so,' Jez agreed in her indolent, dreamy fashion, 'but unfortunately there are complications. In the first place, if you came to the conclusion that someone had been mean enough to want to kill you, you're bound to start wondering about all the mean people you know and asking yourself which one it could have been. If you also happen to have received some threatening letters, it becomes more fraught than ever.'

'Implying that she suspects Desmond of putting poison in Jeremy's champagne? But how? He'd left hours before.'

'Or, more accurately, no one saw him again, which doesn't prove a thing. Those hearty lads weren't to know it, but it's a great pity that one of them didn't accompany him all the way to London. Then we could forget the idea that he might have hung around and bribed one of the waiters to swop clothes with him, making out it was all some jolly lark.'

'Whose idea was that?'

'I forget. Jeremy's maybe, or perhaps I got it from Bert. I gather it's a tale that's going the rounds.'

'But if it were true, someone would have recognised him.'

'Not necessarily, Tess. Very few people actually look at a waiter's face, only at what he's serving them. I checked that out with Bert and he agrees with me. Also the light was very dim in that old tent and Desmond has had lots of experience with make-up. I dare say he might have managed it, so long as he kept out of Ellen's way, which would have been no problem, her being so conspicuously attired on that occasion.'

'And do you honestly consider Desmond to be capable of such a thing?'

'Not on his normal days, no; but he does have these ghastly bouts of rage and depression when he's on the bottle. They don't last long, as a rule, but it practically amounts to insanity when he's in them.'

Turning all this over in my mind, I stared down at one of the charts Jez had been working on when I interrupted her. It consisted of a large sheet of white drawing paper and depicted a huge golden sun with spikes sticking out of it, like a bicycle wheel. Between each spoke there were words and symbols, delicately penned in different coloured inks and, surrounding them like satellites, the twelve signs of the zodiac, also finely illustrated. I found it rather beautiful, but totally meaningless and, dropping it back on the table, I said:

'Do you think it should be followed up?'

'How?'

'Well, for instance, it wouldn't be too difficult to find out exactly what became of Desmond after he was thrown out of the church.'

'For the police to find out, you mean?'

'That would be one way. If he had been innocently amusing himself in London there would probably be witnesses to prove it.'

'I agree with you, up to a point,' Jez admitted. 'It might dispose of one complication, but in principle I'm against it.'

'In principle, or on?'

'Oh, in, because, you see, it's not as simple as it sounds. If Desmond couldn't rake up an alibi, and which of us could on demand, they might easily haul him in for questioning, whether he's guilty, or innocent as a newborn baby. So even if they then turned him loose again, it wouldn't do much to help his career or reputation, both of which are pretty dodgy at the best of times. Ellen would have a hard time reconciling herself to the fact that she was to blame for it, specially as she fells partly responsible for the mess he's in already.'

'How about if he were guilty?'

'That really would be the finish of him, wouldn't it? And she might blame herself even more. Well, you know what she's like, just as well as I do, Tess. She has this exaggerated protective sense about people she's fond of. Comes from indulging Toby all her life, I dare say; but they pretty soon find it out and exert a kind of moral blackmail. It's no good arguing about whether it's right or wrong. It's a built-in feature of her personality and she can't go against it.'

'I dare say she might learn to, in time,' I said. 'It might be less damaging to her personality, in the end, than living with the knowledge that he had once tried to kill either her or Jeremy and could one day take it into his head to do so again.'

Jez shook her head. 'No, I don't suppose she believes there's much danger of that. It's all very ephemeral with Desmond and his moods never last. Besides, Tessa, one has to think these things through, you know, and there's one possible outcome which may not even have occurred to Ellen yet, but which could be completely disastrous from her point of view.'

'What could that be?'

'Well, supposing it did turn out that Desmond was miles away from Roakes when Irene died, wouldn't we then have to take it that she really was the one the murderer was after, all the time? It's rather too much to swallow that there are two people around with a motive for knocking off Ellen or Jeremy.'

'What's so terrible about that? Personally, I'd feel highly relieved if it were true.'

'Then you're not using your loaf because it would have to mean that someone in that small group around Irene had killed her deliberately and, when I told you that Ellen had implicit faith in Jeremy's inability to cause her any harm in any circumstances, I meant just that and no more.'

'So?'

'So I didn't say, did I, that she believed Jeremy to be incapable of murdering someone else?'

CHAPTER THREE

1

THE inquest was scheduled to open in the Coroner's Court at Stadhampton on Wednesday morning and the funeral to be held the following day at Reading Crematorium. This would require Osgood to spend at least three nights in England and a room had been reserved for him at the Swan. Early on Tuesday morning, which was the day following my mildly shattering conversation with Jezebel, I did the civil thing and telephoned the hotel to find out if Mr Lewis had arrived and was in need of comfort or assistance.

After the usual delays I was connected to his room and when I had identified myself and expressed my sympathy, I mentioned that I should be lunching in his neighbourhood and could, if he so desired, call in at the Swan for a few minutes around mid-day and fill him in with whatever he might wish to hear concerning the sad event which had brought him to this country.

This was bending the truth a little, but I still considered that the best solution to our problems rested on the premise of Osgood having murdered Irene by remote control and this was as good a pretext as I could think of for setting out to establish it.

He replied in a soft, rather melodious but subdued voice, perfectly in keeping with the emotions of a bereaved husband and also with the demeanour that any husband with a grain of sense would be at pains to adopt if he had happened to drop a lethal dose in his wife's aspirin bottle, so it was a step neither forward nor backward.

The church clock was booming out the mid-day chimes when I crossed over the bridge into Stadhampton and from that vantage point I could see a score or so of people sitting below me on the hotel's unnaturally brilliant green lawn beside the river. However, when I enquired of the receptionist whether I should find Mr Lewis there, he informed me that he had been requested by Mr Lewis to convey his apologies and to ask me to postpone my appointment with him until after lunch.

'Oh, why's that?' I asked. 'Did he have to go out?'

'No, madam,' the reception clerk replied primly. 'A gentleman called about half-an-hour ago to see him.'

'So he is still in the hotel?'

'Yes, madam. The gentleman asked to be shown to a room where they could talk in private. They are in the television lounge, but I have instructions not to disturb them. Perhaps you would care to leave a message?'

'You don't happen to know the gentleman's name?'

'Couldn't say, I'm afraid,' he replied, snapping his mouth shut so firmly that I felt sure he must be fearful of its betraying him and letting the name out before he could stop it. However, two could play at that game and I said:

'Well, that's a bore because I've come all the way from London and I'm far too early for my next appointment. I'd better clean up a bit and then go and have a drink in your bar. Could you tell me where I'd find the Ladies'?'

'First floor, turn left and then up three more stairs. You'll see the arrow.'

'Thanks very much. Oh, and by the way, please tell Mr Lewis that I'll be back at two-thirty.'

Reaching the first floor, I turned right and marched down the corridor to the door facing me at the end of it, which was labelled 'Residents Only'. I opened it and walked inside, then halted in my tracks, wearing the startled look of a Resident who had set out to watch her favourite television programme and found herself intruding on a private discussion. The act was rendered slightly more realistic by the fact that I had been expecting to see two people and in fact there were three, two men and a woman.

One of the men, the elder of the two, was tall, plump and well-fed looking and was dressed in a suit of royal blue. He also had blue eyes, rather a long nose, soft brown babyish hair growing low on his forehead and a receding double chin. I identified him as Osgood, on the very simple grounds that the other man could only possibly have been a plain-clothes policeman.

The woman was youngish, about thirty-five, well-dressed, dark-haired and attractive, in a kind of super-efficient way, not unlike a younger Stella Roxburgh. I assumed from her presence that Osgood was one of those high-powered executive types who always took his secretary with him on trips abroad and also that this one was the type to command instant attention from airline officials and hotel staffs the world over. The real surprise was that Irene should have tolerated the arrangement.

The C.I.D. man had his back to the window and was the first to become aware of my presence.

'Can I help you?' he enquired mildly.

Osgood swung round in his chair, flinging one arm over the back of it, and favoured me with a broad smile, which just escaped being insolent by virtue of its friendliness. I saw then that Irene might have other problems to contend with, in addition to good-looking secretaries.

'Oh no . . . terribly sorry . . . looking for someone . . . must have come to the wrong . . .' I answered in a great flurry of shy confusion, at the same time backing out of the room and closing the door behind me before any more questions could be asked. I then skipped off down the corridor towards the arrow on the staircase.

The immediate reaction to this encounter was one of pessimism, which had not lifted when I left the hotel some twenty minutes later and started on my way up through the country lanes to Roakes Common. Notwithstanding the temptation to preen myself on having discovered at one stroke the identity of Osgood's visitor, as well as the sort of man I should be contending with at half-past two that afternoon, there was no blinking the fact that here we had a very smooth character indeed, nor the strong indications that neither I, any more than the local C.I.D., had a ghost's chance of getting him to part with one single item of information which he might prefer to keep to himself.

2

There was a laundry van, with its motor running, outside the Ropers' house and Alison was standing at the gate, apparently haranguing the driver. She had an unfortunate habit of browbeating people, usually the wrong people, whether or not she was in the right and, as a result, invariably lost not only her case, but every vestige of sympathy as well. The pattern appeared to be repeating itself now, for the driver abruptly put his foot down on the accelerator and drove off, leaving her open-mouthed and still in mid-flow.

'Having trouble?' I asked, winding down my window.

'You can say that again! It's getting beyond a joke. Two sheets missing this week and a towel the week before; and half the stuff is torn to ribbons when it does come back. I was telling him, it's simply not good enough, but he couldn't care less.'

'Bad luck! Why not switch to another firm?'

'Are you joking? How many laundries do you imagine deliver up in this neck of the woods? A launderette would be the answer, but how am I expected to lug all the stuff down to Stadhampton without a car?'

'Couldn't Phil take it for you?'

'Oh, he would like a shot, if I were to ask him, specially now he's home for the long vac, but it's not really on for a bloke of his age to be lumbered with all these domestic chores.'

'Good practice for when he gets married. Is he at home now?'

'Yes, tinkering about with the old bus, as per. He's fixing it up with a radio now, that's the latest craze. And what brings you to these parts? Not on your way to visit his lordship, I trust?'

'I had thought of calling there, yes. In fact, I was hoping to cadge some lunch.'

'Then you're out of luck, my dear. He's gone up to town for the day. Or so Mrs Parkes told me when I happened to run into her at the butcher's just now.'

'Oh, damn! And that probably means he was intending to lunch with me in London. What a fearful breakdown in communications. Oh well, can't be helped, I suppose.'

'Can't even offer you pot luck here, I'm afraid. Phil's going to put in some rowing practice this afternoon, so he'll have his main meal this evening and I never bother with lunch when I'm on my own.'

'Tell you what, then, Alison, why don't we both go up to the pub and get a sandwich? Come on! Do you good to get out for a bit.'

'Well, it sounds a nice idea, but you don't want to be stuck with my boring company.'

This was true, in a sense, but I still had more than an hour to kill and the prospect of spending it on my own at the Bricklayers' was even less alluring, so I piled on the pressure until she gave in, although this was only achieved on the strict understanding that it should be a Dutch treat.

Predictably enough, the conversation revolved mainly around Phil and over her second glass of barley wine Alison's obsessive concern for him took an even more confidential turn. She had been telling me how he was still reeling under the blow of Ellen's defection and how all her efforts to persuade him to go out and mix with other young people had been ignored, and she added,

'Of course we know it's a dodgy time, waiting for the exam results to come in, but all he ever wants to do nowadays is tinker about with the old Mini, or else spend hours on his own, sculling on the river. It's not healthy for a lad of his age, is it?'

'At his age, though, he'll soon snap out of it.'

'That's all very fine, but I'd like to know how. And he doesn't confide in me as he used to, that's another headache.'

'How do you know he doesn't?'

'Well, take yesterday, for example.'

'What happened yesterday?'

'He told me he was going up to London to interview for a job at one of those holiday camps. Compères or something, I think they call themselves.'

Although it was hard to imagine Phil shining very brightly in this role, I considered that the urge to try it was a promising sign, but when I mentioned this she said:

'Oh granted, and I was pleased as Punch when he told me, you can bet your bottom dollar on that. But it wasn't the real reason he went to London. He never said a word about it when he got home, and when I asked him how he'd got on he just went off into one of his quiet moods.'

'So what did he really go for? Did you discover?'

'It's not cricket to discuss him behind his back, really,' Alison replied, which was rather a startling observation in view of the fact that she scarcely ever did anything else. 'But it's been worrying me more than somewhat,' she went on, having overcome her scruples with another fortifying intake of barley wine, 'and I'd jolly well like to get to the bottom of it. I dare not ask Phil outright. He's so touchy these days, he'd probably blow his top, but you've met this chap and you may have a clue about what's behind it.'

'Behind what? What chap?' I asked, greatly mystified.

'That actor who used to be a friend of Ellen's. Desmond something or other.'

'Desmond Davidson? But what's the connection between him and Phil? I didn't know they'd even met.'

'Oh, I think Phil may have come across him once or twice when Ellen brought him down here to stay with her father, although he tried to keep out of their way as much as he could, poor old dear! Still, that doesn't explain why they should be meeting each other in London and Phil not telling me a word about it, does it?'

'No, it doesn't, but how did you find out?'

'Well, it was bad luck on Phil really. He hadn't left the house above ten minutes when the phone rang and it was this Desmond asking for him. I told him Phil had gone up to London and he said it was too bad because they'd got an appointment to meet at some pub in Soho and he was going to be late getting there, or something of the kind. I forget the details. I was so taken aback I could hardly take in what he was saying.'

'But he told you who he was?'

'No, he didn't and he rang off without giving me the chance to ask him; but I knew all right. Holiday camp officials don't interview their applicants in Soho pubs, for a start. Besides, there's no mistaking that voice, is there?'

This was true, for Desmond's gravelly voice, with its occasional, carefully cultivated break, was one of his principal charms.

'Someone took me to see a play he was in at Oxford not long ago,' Alison explained, 'and he's been on the box dozens of times, so I knew who he was all right. Trouble was, I was caught on the hop and I couldn't collect myself fast enough to ask what it was all about. I suppose you haven't any idea?'

'Not really. The only explanation that occurs to me is that Phil feels he has more in common with Desmond than anyone else just now. You know, two lonely hearts broken by the same girl kind of stuff. It would make a bond, I suppose.'

To my relief, she seized on this theory and began enlarging on it and finding means to make it more credible, ignoring or oblivious of the fact that Desmond was far too conceited to place himself on the same level as an obscure young man like Phil, or to view their situations as in any way comparable.

However, I encouraged her to work away on this solution, considering it wiser, both for her sake as well as Phil's, that she should be spared an inkling of what had struck me as the true explanation as soon as the subject had been broached. It had brought back the memory of a conversation I had had with Phil at the wedding reception, and of the puzzled and mutinous expression on his face as he insisted on there being something bogus and potentially sinister about one of the waiters. The latest revelation suggested that he had come to the same conclusion as Ellen as to whose death by poison had really been plotted and by whom, and had set out to do a little private sleuthing on his own.

'If I were you, I'd let it ride,' I told Alison, who had temporarily run out of comforting theories of her own invention. 'This friendship, or whatever, will soon fizzle out and in the meantime it will be no end of a boost to Phil's morale to suffer in such illustrious company.'

Her next words would have startled Jez far less than they did me, for they merely proved that whatever guards you may put on your tongue, you cannot control the thought waves and E.S.P.s, which continue to hop around in the atmosphere in the most unbridled fashion. She said,

'Of course it's been a difficult time all round, with that dreadful business of Irene coming on top of all the other trials. It hasn't been too pleasant having the police invading the place, without any warning, to go nosing through her room and pester us with more questions. They ought to realise by now that there's nothing more we can tell them. At least, that is . . .'

'What?'

'Well, it's funny, and I wouldn't have expected anyone but me to have noticed, but once or twice I've caught Phil with that look on his face which usually means he's going to blurt something out which will send us all up in smoke; but it never happened. If he has got something on his mind, he's keeping it to himself and it wouldn't be any use my asking him about it.'

'All the same, I'd have a go,' I advised her. 'If there's any single thing, however tiny, that he knows and the police don't, he really ought to pass it on.'

'All very well to say that and I dare say you're right, but he lacks confidence, that's always been Phil's trouble, and he'd be scared of making a fool of himself.'

'Oh, but that's nonsense, it really is. You can quote me, if you like, Alison, because I do know that when the police are working like this, more or less in the dark, every scrap of information is pounced on as though it were pure gold, and he needn't be afraid they won't take him seriously, even if it does turn out to be irrelevant.'

I was wholly sincere in handing out this advice, but the urgency with which I strove to impress it upon Alison was more for her benefit and Phil's than to smooth the path of justice. I was convinced that life would be a lot safer for both of them if they would only follow it.

CHAPTER FOUR

'SO WE meet again!' Osgood said, half-rising from his chair in the restaurant, which was the most that the space between his and the next table would allow. 'What a pleasant surprise. Do come and join us.'

I had been directed to the dining room, which was crowded as usual, but had found no difficulty in picking him out, for Osgood evidently knew his way around and he and his presumed secretary were occupying one of the most sought after tables by the window, commanding a fine view of the garden and weir. They were drinking coffee and liqueurs and I accepted the first and declined the second, having already gone slightly over my quota while listening to Alison's tale of woe. On this occasion, however, abstinence did not pay off, for nothing less than a treble brandy could have inured me to the shock of his next remarks, which were as follows:

'This is Mrs Price, dearie,' he said, addressing the female companion, 'who's been good enough to come all the way down here to tell us about poor Irene. Mrs Price, my wife!'

Since he had specifically referred to Irene, there could be no question of mistaken identity and it was lucky for me that that waiter had already arrived with my coffee, enabling me to get through the next couple of minutes in a twitter of indecision as to whether to drink it with or without milk. At the end of this breathtaking performance, I got yet another reprieve, for dearie pushed her chair back, saying,

'If you two will excuse me, I think I'll go and take a nap. Don't think me rude, but I know you have things to discuss which don't entirely concern me and it'll maybe make it easier for both of you to have me out of the way.'

The counter protestations and jumping around which ensued gave me ample opportunity to regain total *sang froid* and I seated myself once more, fully able to return Osgood's bland and knowing smile with the requisite coolness.

'Anything wrong?' he enquired, obviously much amused.

'Absolutely nothing, thank you.'

'Coffee just as you like it?'

'Yes, thanks, everything's fine. Well no, why should I keep this up? I obviously didn't fool you for one minute. The truth is, I was really knocked sideways when you introduced . . .'

'Jay.'

'As your wife.'

'Well, why not? She is my wife.'

'Forgive my saying so, Mr Lewis, but I'm rather puzzled. Are you a Muslim or something?'

'No, we were married in a Christian church, if that's your worry.'

'It isn't. What worries me is what you might call the time factor. You can't have been a widower for more than twenty-four hours.'

'Wrong. I've never been a widower,' he replied in his gentle, languid voice, 'I was divorced for a year or so, but that was a long way back. Jay and I have been married almost three years. We have an eighteen-month-old son to prove it.'

'You're not pulling my leg? You really are saying that you weren't Irene's husband anymore? But she never told us! When she cabled that she was coming over for the wedding she simply said she'd be on her own because you were tied up.'

'Which was substantially more accurate than many of the things she said, you have to admit?'

'She also said that you sent your regards.'

'So I did, and where's the harm in that? Look, how about changing your mind and having that brandy, after all? I'm going to order another for me and I hate drinking alone.'

Without waiting for my reply, he raised his left hand by about three centimetres and a waiter arrived at the gallop.

'I used to have to see Irene from time to time,' he explained when the order had been given. 'For one thing, she was in constant need of advice over her financial affairs or pretended to be. The real truth was that she hated to let go, poor girl, and she considered that I had an obligation to get her out of each and every jam. I suppose it was justified in a way because if I hadn't given her the money in the first place she wouldn't have found so many ways of losing it.'

'Alimony, do you mean?'

'No, I'm referring to a fairly substantial sum I settled on her when we were first married and she could have asked for the moon and got it, if she'd cared to. There was never a question of alimony. At that time she didn't need it and furthermore I was the one to start divorce proceedings.'

'On what grounds? Or is that an impertinent question?'

'No, it's very pertinent, but I thought you'd come here to tell me things, not to ask them?'

'I know, but you must realise that the situation is so different from what we'd all been led to believe. Still, it's no business of mine, I agree.'

'Now, now! Stop being prim with me and drink up your brandy,' he said, giving my hand a friendly pat. 'If Jay were here, she'd tell you that I never can resist teasing people I like and I certainly don't have any objection to telling you why Irene and I came unstuck. It's down in the records as incompatibility, mental cruelty and a few other things, but the main reason was that she always refused to have a child. It didn't seem to matter in the early days, but later on, after the glory had faded and she'd begun sleeping around, there was really nothing to hold us together.'

'Why did she refuse?'

'She claimed it was on her doctor's orders. Even in my infatuated period I took that with a grain of salt, since having Ellen didn't seem to have done her any harm, although she kept it from me for as long as she could that she already had one child. I suppose the real reason was she was scared of losing her figure.'

'It doesn't sound as though you had many illusions about her,' I remarked. 'Which is no particular surprise. What I don't understand is why you troubled to come here at all. No one could have compelled you to, in the circumstances.'

'Well, don't run away with the idea that it was sheer altruism. I have various business interests in Europe, so it's never hard to find an excuse to fly over. And Jay's always been promised a trip to Paris as soon as the boy was old enough to be left with her parents. We'll probably spend a week there before we go home.'

'Nevertheless, you came at very short notice, did you not? Can't have given yourself very much time to set up any business deals?'

Osgood was lighting a fresh cigar and he swivelled his eyes sideways without moving his head.

'You're very pertinacious, aren't you, young lady?'

'Inquisitive, you mean?'

'If you like,' he replied after a few experimental puffs. 'No, pertinacious is really the better word, and it does cause me to wonder where your own interest lies. Not in affection for my ex-wife, I take it?'

'No, I scarcely knew her.'

'So there's something else on your mind? Well, I've no objection to helping you shift it if you think that delving into my motives will get you anywhere. I told you I was no altruist, but the kind of feeling I had for Irene when I first knew her doesn't just fade away and leave no trace. I still felt responsible for her, up to a point, and she damn well saw to it that I should. When the police contacted me and told me she had died suddenly and in suspicious circumstances, it didn't take more than a minute to figure out that she hadn't seen fit to let on that we'd been divorced for six years. That seemed kind of sad; pathetic, if you know what I mean? That tremendous vanity of hers wasn't going to allow any of you lot to see her as rejected and unloved. She had to be on top all the time, envied and admired by all the lesser breeds. So there she was, poor little devil, ending her life among a bunch of strangers who didn't give a damn about her, didn't even know one single truth about how things really were for her.'

'That was her fault, not ours.'

'I know that, and I'm not making excuses for her, but just the same it seemed to me a sad way to go. That's what decided me to drop everything and come over and Jay, being the sport she is, came along for the ride. Satisfied?'

'Yes, but it's all bad news, so far as I'm concerned.'

'So you'd set me up as the villain of the piece and now you've found it won't stick, is that the problem?'

'Now you're being pertinacious?'

'Oh, I have my moments, but I wouldn't call this one of them. That little talk I had with the local cop this morning cleared a few mists. I was expecting him to start digging for facts about Irene's medical history, but not on your life! It was her state of mind he was interested in. There could only be one reason for that and I had to tell him that in my view suicide was out.'

'Which was true?'

'Don't you believe me?'

'Yes.'

'Her life may have been folding up on her in some departments, and she was starting to compensate with too much alcohol and too many pills, but that's not uncommon in women of her type and she was nowhere near the stage of bowing out. The world still contained rich men, she could still look beautiful in a good light and she hadn't given up, by any means. In fact, I'd say she took better care of herself than most.'

'You're not doing much to cheer me up,' I remarked.

'I see it, and if I'd known it would hit you like this I might have been tempted to say she threatened suicide every hour on the hour. I'm a kind-hearted man and nothing works on me like beauty in distress.'

'Thank you, but it's too late to think of that now.'

'Yes, it is and it wouldn't have done us any good, you know. They'd have checked my story and they wouldn't have found another person in the whole wide world to back it up. All of which could have landed me in trouble and I'm not that kind-hearted.'

'Why could it have?'

'Well, look now, as things stand, I'm out of it: divorced, remarried, new home and family, no financial or emotional involvement with my ex, nothing to gain by her death. That's fine, from my point of view, but the minute I start inventing tales which have no foundation, trying to mislead people, the picture changes, doesn't it? So maybe after all I did have some motive for slipping a dose of poison in among Irene's pills and maybe it wouldn't hurt to try and uncover it. They wouldn't find anything, but just looking and maybe dragging Jay into it could be unpleasant enough.'

'So he told you all that, did he? That the poison could have been in her pills?'

'Sure, why not? I'm the innocent party, who's come forward of his own free will to help sort things out. Naturally I'd be curious to know how she died and what's to prevent him telling me?'

'And you can't think of anyone else, anyone in Canada, I mean, who might have wanted her not to come back?'

'Not a chance. Mind you, I'm not saying she was loved by one and all. She was very inquisitive on certain levels and she had a bad trick of nosing out dirty little secrets and spreading them around where they'd do the most harm. So naturally she didn't have too many friends. So what? Why should anyone bother to take that kind of risk when all they needed was to keep out of her way? In fact,

I'd say the real tragedy of Irene was that no one honestly cared a damn whether she lived or died. I assume from your concern that the position was a little different on your side of the Atlantic?'

'True, but it's more complicated than that.'

'My goodness, you do carry a load on those frail shoulders! It sounds as though poor Irene is creating as much mayhem now as she did during her misspent life.'

'It's not altogether her fault. In fact, there's a school of thought that rejects the idea that the poison was ever intended for her and I must admit that what you've told me rather strengthens that theory. Still, I've no right to burden you with my problems.'

I confess to a certain insincerity here because in the first place there was no evidence that the burden was wearing him into an early grave and also he had all the charm of a good listener, which made talking to him a pleasure. I hoped to have said just enough to keep his curiosity alive, which must have been the case, for he said,

'It sounds to me as though you need to burden someone with them and I have all the time in the world until Jay is ready to surface again. You could begin by showing me how I've contributed to this theory and what it's based on.'

'Well, you see, there's always the possibility that the poison was in one of the glasses and, if so, that Irene got it by mistake, and that narrows the suspects down to a tiny group of people who were all present at the time. I'd been hoping, you see, that it would turn out that someone in Canada had a beautiful motive for murdering her, but was nowhere near when it happened.'

'That someone being myself?' Osgood asked, sounding perfectly friendly about it.

'Well yes, I must confess that you would have done nicely. I should apologise for that, I suppose, but I got the idea before I met you and found out the truth about your marriage. If only it had turned out that she'd got all the money and was refusing to divorce you or something of that kind, it would have been plain sailing. If it makes it any better, I should add that, having met you, I no longer believe you would be capable of such a mean trick, whatever the circumstances, but I wasn't to know that, was I?'

'No, but I accept the compliment and I congratulate you.'

'Whatever for?'

'For putting it so nicely that I end up feeling indebted. Something like the prisoner in the box must feel towards the judge who's sentenced him to five years when he was expecting life. So how can I show my gratitude?'

'I don't see any way, frankly. The big trouble is that it's almost inconceivable that anyone in this country could have felt a strong enough animosity towards Irene to want to murder her. Most of the people involved were meeting her for the first time and not one had set eyes on her for fifteen years. Besides, what the hell? She was due to fly back to Winnipeg the day after the wedding.'

'You know that for a fact?'

'Well no, since you ask, I suppose I simply took it for granted, but the people she was staying with down here certainly weren't expecting to keep her for one more night and, as far as I know, she had no reason to remain in England.'

'She could have found one.'

'Such as?'

'Well, life back home hadn't been all that exciting recently. If she'd seen the chance of a comfortable berth over here, she might have been planning to stay and work on it.'

'Another rich husband, do you mean?'

'Or someone else's rich husband. It's hard to say, but if I were you I wouldn't rule out the possibility that she was getting in someone's hair, or threatening to. It would be just like her.'

It was also just about the most unwelcome advice he could have given me and it says a lot for his personality that even at that moment I felt no personal resentment. In fact, I found myself thinking that in some ways he rather reminded me of Robin.

CHAPTER FIVE

1

THE inquest opened at eleven sharp on Wednesday morning and closed again precisely ten minutes later, the police having requested an adjournment, pending further enquiries. Formal identification was made by Osgood and the cause of death established as poisoning by paraquat and back in London again that evening Robin told me that Scotland Yard had been asked to help in the investigation. Naturally enough, he had not been invited to work on the case which was to be handled by Detective Superintendent Powell, a member of the old brigade, for whom Robin had respect, but no special affection.

Toby was eventually badgered into attending the cremation ceremony and was supported on one side by Dr Macintosh and on the other by Jeremy. Robin also managed to snatch time to swell the pathetic numbers and he told me afterwards that Osgood had been present, though not Jay, and that Alison had sent a wreath, which was remarkably handsome of her, in view of her straitened circumstances and probably proof that she was the only one of us who had felt any genuine liking for Irene and truly regretted her death.

Ellen also stayed away and, seeing this as a rare chance for a private consultation with her, I went round to Hans Place as soon as the cortège had started on its way.

I found her at the ironing board, battling with one of Jeremy's shirts and presenting such a fairy tale image of the wee bride in her first home that it required an effort to remember that her mother had recently been violently done to death and that she lived in dread of the same thing happening to her husband.

However, I was not given much time to dwell on this irony, for someone else had also gambled on its being a propitious moment to catch Ellen on her own and she had no sooner put the ironing board away and filled the coffee percolator than the front door bell rang. I went to answer it for her and found Superintendent Powell and his underling, Sergeant Blaikie, standing on the mat.

His request was for a few words in private, but Ellen implored him to let me stay and hear them as well and she looked so pitiful and appealing that his stony heart visibly melted.

'She is my cousin, after all, and she's very discreet, you know,' Ellen told him.

'Oh yes?' he replied, looking at me sourly and getting a question mark into it.

'Besides, there's nothing I can tell you that she doesn't know already.'

This was obviously a rather more cogent argument than the previous one and the superintendent made no further objection. Ellen tripped back to the kitchen, accompanied by the sergeant, who had been commanded in a meaning voice to give a hand by carrying the tray.

'Nice and quiet round here,' the superintendent then remarked, having cleared his throat once or twice and strolled in a nonchalant manner to the window.

'Not bad,' I admitted. 'Where do you live, by the way?'

'Parsons Green, if you know where that is? None of your posh Knightsbridge,' he added aggressively.

'That must be fairly quiet too,' I said, hoping that Ellen wouldn't start chatting up the sergeant and forget to press on with the coffee.

'Are you acting in anything at present, then, Mrs Price?'

'Not just at the moment. I'm between productions.'

'Ah! What they call resting. Lot of that in your profession, I understand?'

'Quite a lot, yes. Are you keen on the theatre?'

'So so. Can't take too much of this modern stuff, though. I like something I can get my teeth into. Shaw, Ibsen, that lot. Something to make you think, if you know what I mean?'

'Yes, I know exactly what you mean.'

'Still, I suppose you get around a bit, see a good many stage people and all that, even when you're resting?' he suggested, with such studied offhandedness as to warn me that the light banter was now over and we were skating round a subject near to his heart, although I could not imagine what it might be, unless by ill chance he belonged to those legions whose niece had written a play.

'Well yes,' I agreed cautiously. 'I've got a few friends in the business, naturally. Most of them are struggling actors like myself.'

'Ever come across one named Desmond Davidson?' he asked, with another onrush of calculated casualness.

When my mind had completed a couple of twirls, I endeavoured to kill his act by saying cheerfully,

'Oh, frequently. We were in a play together at Nottingham about two years ago.'

'Is that when he met Mrs Roxburgh?'

For a moment I thought he was talking about Stella and was wrestling with this new complication when it came to me that he was referring to Ellen.

'Yes,' I agreed, pretending to have been considering the matter from all angles, 'I suppose it must have been. I do remember that she came up and spent a weekend with me during the run. Why do you ask?'

'What sort of character is he, in your opinion?' the superintendent asked, ignoring my question, as I had expected.

'It's probably the same as most people's. He can be very good, brilliant on occasions, but he's too uneven and undisciplined to hit the heights, and he's bad at taking direction. Always thinks he knows best how a scene should be played and it often involves everyone else standing about with their backs to the audience.'

'Oh, I'm afraid I'm out of my depth now, Mrs Price. These technical details are above my head. What I wanted was your assessment of his character.'

'I realise that and what I've told you isn't irrelevant because, in so far as he exists off stage, the pattern is identical. He can be very generous and affectionate, but he's too volatile and egotistic to sustain a deep friendship and he's permanently at the mercy of his moods. I hope that helps?'

'Maybe. Anything else occur to you?'

'He's rather given to practical jokes during certain of these moods.'

'Is he now?' the superintendent asked, allowing a gleam of genuine interest to peep through for the first time, but no opportunity to follow this up was granted to him, for the door was flung wide and the coffee makers returned, Sergeant Blaikie virtuously carrying the tray. It was plain from his superior's irritable expression that he had jumped his cue, but, no bugging devices having been wired up in the kitchen, he could scarcely be blamed for that.

'Do you like milk and sugar in yours?' Ellen asked.

'A dash of both, please,' Superintendent Powell replied and then, as she brought the cup over to him and placed it on the table by the window, his hand went to his pocket and produced a sheet of writing paper, which he flashed in front of her nose, saying,

'Do you recognise this, Mrs Roxburgh?'

If he had been relying on shock tactics to get results, he may have been gratified by their effect, although it was a hollow victory, for Ellen took one look at the letter, let out a small scream and fell to the floor in a dead faint.

I was afraid it would not do her much good and I was right, for although the sergeant looked very guilty and bothered, as he helped me lift her on to the sofa, the odious Powell merely sighed, put the sheet of paper on the table and wearily picked up his coffee cup.

As though sensing that her performance had fallen rather flat, Ellen opened her eyes after a couple of minutes, though not omitting to put the conventional question in the conventionally petulant voice.

'Right here, just where you were two minutes ago,' I assured her. 'And all the same people are still here with you. How would it be if you were to lie still for a bit, while I look around for the burnt feathers?' I suggested, in case she needed further time.

However, this appeared not to be the case for she sat up smiling weakly like a true little heroine and said in a brave voice:

'No, I'll be all right now. Sorry to be so stupid. How did you come by that letter?' she asked the superintendent in slightly stronger tones.

'I'll come to that in a moment,' he replied, picking it up again. 'First of all, there are one or two questions I'd like to put to you, if you're sure you're feeling well enough?'

'Oh yes, thanks, I think I'll be all right now.'

'Then am I correct in believing that you recognised this handwriting?'

'Yes, of course you are, no one could mistake it.'

'And also that you had seen this particular letter before?'

'No, not as far as I know.'

'I beg your pardon? Could you repeat that?'

'I said "not as far as I know", but of course I didn't have a chance to study it at all carefully.'

'Then perhaps you would kindly do so now?'

She nodded and the superintendent handed the letter to the sergeant, who brought it reverently to the sofa.

It was a single sheet, covered on both sides with large, flamboyant script, liberally scattered with dashes, capital letters and underlinings, such as Queen Victoria would have felt quite at home with, but although Ellen obligingly spread it out flat on her lap I was unable to decipher more than an odd word or two, not enough to get even the gist of its message.

She read it through very slowly, glancing up at me briefly as she turned the page to begin on the reverse side, and when it was done folded the sheet again and held it out to the sergeant for the first lap of its return journey.

'All quite clear now?' the superintendent asked.

'Yes, thank you.'

'And you recognise the handwriting?'

'Yes, I've told you that. It was written by a man named Desmond Davidson that I used to see a lot of before my marriage. It's signed with the initial "D", as you probably saw.'

'And would you mind telling me when this particular letter was written?'

'I'm afraid I have no idea,' Ellen replied in a startled voice. 'Was there no date on it? I didn't notice.'

The superintendent opened his mouth, then paused to rub the back of his thumb against his chin, while she regarded him with a bright, enquiring look.

'Let me re-phrase the question, Mrs Roxburgh: do you recall when it was you received this letter?'

'I?' she asked in great astonishment.

'Yes, you. You won't deny that it was addressed to you?'

'Oh, but I will. At any rate, I never received it and I don't know why you should imagine that I did. It doesn't start "Dear Ellen", or anything like that.'

'True, but then you'll agree that it is hardly written in the conventional form?'

'Yes, very strange, I do agree with you there,' Ellen said placidly. 'But I fail to understand why you should deduce from that that it was written to me. What is the connection?'

'We assumed as much from information received, and I would draw your attention to the fact that the name Jeremy is mentioned several times in connection with various threats and invective. I take it you won't deny that Jeremy is your husband's name?'

'No, of course not, but there are hundreds of Jeremys around. I can't be responsible for all of them.'

'No, only for the one that this Mr Davidson appears to have got his knife into, on grounds of somewhat fanatical jealousy. It would be rather a coincidence, would it not, if there were two separate men who fitted into that category and they were both called Jeremy?'

'Yes, it would, but why should there be two? I feel sure there is only one and you have got the wrong one. My husband and Mr Davidson have always been on excellent terms. They were at school together and, as far as I know, there has never been a cross word.'

'Even when you ended your association with Mr Davidson and became engaged to marry Mr Roxburgh?'

'Oh, certainly. Desmond was delighted. It was he who introduced us, and our association, as you call it, had never included the possibility of marriage.'

'I must ask you to forgive my saying so, Mrs Roxburgh, but I find that hard to believe.'

'Ask him!' Ellen said smoothly. 'I am sure he will tell you the same thing.'

Once again the superintendent paused for some chin nibbing before proceeding and his voice, when he did so, had taken on a new note of hostility:

'Yes, no doubt he would. Our informant, I must tell you . . .'

'Oh yes, your informant? You were going to tell me who it was and how you came into possession of that letter.'

'On the contrary, madam. Since you have decided not to cooperate with us, I may as well say frankly that I have no intention of giving you that information.'

'Oh, very well, then I must learn to live without it, but I can't be expected to make things up just to suit you, can I?'

'No, I confess that I had not expected you to, and if you'll accept a word of advice, you'll consider your position very carefully. If you change your mind or get any fresh ideas about this letter, you can always get in touch with me at this number and extension,' he said, bringing out a card and placing it very deliberately on the table. 'Don't get up, we can see ourselves out, but before I go it is only fair to warn you that, whatever your reason for wishing to protect someone, it is likely to lead to the most serious consequences if you persist in taking this obstructive line. Not only for yourself, I must add, but for other people as well. Please remember that.'

2

'Whereupon she promptly did a genuine faint,' I said, when describing the interview to Robin. 'At least, I think it was. She is a great loss to the stage, as you know, but one has to remember that she had a lot on her mind, even before old Powell started handing out ominous threats. On the other hand, of course, she may just have been giving herself a little time to consider what to say to me.'

'And what was that, when she got around to it?'

'Well, first of all, she asked me if it was a criminal offence to withhold evidence.'

'And what did you tell her?'

'That I didn't think so, as long as she wasn't under oath, but that she couldn't expect to get away with it for long. Whatever else Superintendent Powell may be doing, he's certainly not sitting back in his office, saying: "Curse it, foiled again!"'

'Did she have any ideas as to how he got hold of the letter? I presume it was one she'd received from Desmond?'

'Oh yes, there was no point in keeping up that pretence. For one thing, she'd admitted to me on her wedding day that he'd been sending threatening letters.'

'And was there something specially incriminating about this one?'

'Apparently there was. It was by far the wildest of the lot and included the categorical statement that if she insisted on going through with the marriage he would kill Jeremy and then himself.'

'Although, whether or not he set out to kill Jeremy, he has certainly not yet killed himself.'

'Which is mainly why Ellen is so bent on protecting him.'

'Rather a loopy kind of logic?'

'Not really, because she's convinced the whole thing was sheer play-acting and the fact that he hasn't attempted suicide merely confirms that. Whenever Desmond's not being paid to play a part he has to make one up for himself and he throws as much of himself into it as he would if he were in a theatre, but it has no more reality for him than any other performance. He would be just as likely to murder Jeremy in actual fact as to blind himself with a knitting needle in the wings while waiting to go on as Oedipus. On the other hand, she has no illusions about making the police understand this, and apparently the letter really does make him out to be quite a dangerous sort of lunatic.'

'I think she underestimates them. They are not wholly incapable of distinguishing between guilt and exhibitionism.'

'Well, anyway, it's a risk she's not prepared to take. At best, it could be several days and perhaps even a spell in custody before they made the distinction and it could be the end of Desmond. His reputation is sticky enough already, without the suspicion of murder being tacked on to it.'

'So back to my first question: How did the letter land so neatly in the lap of old Father Powell?'

'Why is that so important?'

'Well, someone must have sent it to him and that person either honestly believes Desmond to be guilty, or is going flat out to make it appear so. In which case . . .'

'In which case, that person could very well be the real murderer? I see what you mean.'

'So, from every point of view, it wouldn't hurt to know.'

'Couldn't you just ask Powell?'

'Me? You must be out of your mind, Tessa! It's his case, nothing to do with me, and I'm on particularly shaky ground here, seeing that a number of my relatives are mixed up in it. Besides, what could I do with the information, in the improbable event of his giving it to me? Certainly not pass it on to you or Ellen. Not, that is, unless I had already typed out my letter of resignation.'

'I suppose that's true, but it does seem a shame that he should know something that we don't.'

'I doubt if he does. I should say the chances of this informant having identified himself are a million to one. Little snippets of that kind are invariably sent in anonymously, and that applies just as much to true information as to false. Besides, from your description, it doesn't sound as though Powell was on very sure ground himself. He seems to have blustered a bit, but not to have made any serious attempt to pin Ellen down or frighten her into telling the truth. Incidentally, didn't he show any curiosity about the violence of her reaction when he produced the letter? It was hardly a thing to faint about unless she had something to hide.'

'I think that may have been to save himself embarrassment. Perhaps he thought she was pregnant, but also he'd probably sized her up by that time and realised she was perfectly capable of saying she was. I suppose that, combined with the shock of her mother's death, could have made it seem plausible.'

'Furthermore, despite his solemn warnings, there may even lurk a tiny doubt as to whether she really was lying, so to that extent, at least, you have the advantage of him.'

'Although it's not a very comfortable one to have.'

'Why? Does it shock you to discover that she's such a little fibber?'

'No, not at all. She was lying to protect another person, so it doesn't count. The trouble is, who was she protecting? I assumed it was Desmond, but Ellen's a very sharp number and she could have jumped several paces ahead of me, during the first fainting spell, and come up with the same answer as you did. If so, the one she was protecting has to be Jeremy.'

'Meaning that he first tried to poison her and is now trying to get the blame shifted on to Desmond? That would be quite neat, because if he were to repeat the experiment he would only need to ensure that Desmond was around at the time and the police would have their guilty party all lined up for them.'

'Yes, but Jez won't have any of that. She's convinced that Ellen and Jeremy trust each other implicitly and, with all that intuition and extra-sensory perception to guide her, she could be right. On the other hand, she did hint that Ellen might find it credible that Jeremy could be ruthless enough to kill someone else; only that doesn't make sense because he couldn't possibly have had any motives for wanting Irene out of the way. With all her faults, she wasn't a mother-in-law who would be in and out of the house all day. Oh dear, what a nuisance it is, Robin! What chance have we of finding the murderer when we don't even know who he meant to kill?'

'I still think he or she might be traced through Desmond's letter. I have a feeling that may turn out to have been a rash move on someone's part and that your safest bet is to concentrate on it. By the way, how and when did Ellen receive it?'

'First post, day before the wedding. It arrived at the flat, along with several other letters and some last minute presents.'

'And what was her reaction?'

'What you'd expect. It upset her, naturally; but then she showed it to Jez, who was much inclined to shrug it off, and when they'd talked it over Ellen more or less came round to the same point of view. Immediately afterwards she got caught up in the fuss of wedding preparations, including the fact that her dress was delivered and she didn't think the final alterations had been properly done. So there was hardly time to give the letter another thought.'

'Nevertheless, she kept it? Whether it was to be taken seriously or not, wouldn't it have been wiser to destroy it?'

'I asked her about that and it seems she had meant to do so, but Jez advised her to hang on to it.'

'Why was that?'

'Just in case Desmond continued to make a pest of himself, started ringing up in the middle of the night and things like that. So then, if it got really so bad that she had to get her solicitors to choke him off, she'd be in a much stronger position if she could wave this letter about.'

'So what did she do with it?'

'Put it inside her address book, along with the other letters and cards that had arrived that morning. Not a very sensible move perhaps, but then I suppose it would have been rather a distasteful thing to carry around in one's bag. She left the address book in her bedroom at the flat.'

'Why?'

'Because the Roxburghs were driving her down to the country. She was taking two dress boxes with her and she didn't want to lumber them with a suitcase as well, so there was no convenient way of carrying the address book. She left it for Jeremy to collect, with some other parcels, later in the day. Perhaps it was a trifle indiscreet of her, but she had a lot on her mind and a girl can't be expected to be very clear headed when she's about to float up the aisle. She did take the precaution of telephoning Jez after lunch, to remind her to make sure that Jeremy didn't overlook the address book, but unfortunately she was too late. He'd already called at the flat by then and the book was still there. Jez brought it down herself the next day.'

'Which doesn't preclude the possibility that Jeremy had seen it and read the letter?'

'Nor does it preclude the possibility that dear little Caspar had removed the letter and left it lying around for anyone to read.'

'I can't see why that should matter. Jez must already have known it by heart.'

'Yes, but there's still Bert, who's a great old gossip and, contrary to general belief, spends a good deal of time on the premises, although keeping rather irregular hours. Besides, all sorts of people wander in and out of that flat. To make life more convenient for herself, Jez doesn't even bother to keep the front door properly fastened and when she's closeted in the kitchen, working on the zodiac, anyone could walk in and poke around in the other rooms without her knowing.'

'Though it's hard to see why they should bother, unless it was with that special object in view, which would presumably only apply to Desmond himself. But if, having realised how insane he'd been to write the letter and then set out to retrieve it, he is surely not so unbalanced as to have put it in an envelope addressed to Scotland Yard?'

'There is the remote possibility,' I suggested, 'that Jez took it herself, as a safety measure and then sent it to the police when Irene died. If so, I doubt very much whether she could be prevailed upon to admit it.'

'All this, of course, hinging on the premise that the letter had gone by the time Ellen finally got her hands on the address book?'

'That's what she says, but why did you automatically assume it?'

'Only because it would account for her subsequent behaviour; the dazed mood she was in when you went up to help her change, and the decision to postpone the honeymoon trip.'

'Yes, you're right; and not knowing who had pinched the letter, or for what purpose, would have given rise to all sorts of unpleasant speculations. Naturally, she would have been in no mood for a jolly holiday with all that weighing on her mind. One sees it clearly now.'

'And she has positively no idea who might have taken it?'

'None whatever, so she claims, and if she hasn't I don't see what chance there is for anyone else.'

'Well, bend your mind to it,' Robin advised me. 'Personally I still regard it as largely irrelevant at this stage to worry about who intended to kill whom and for what reason. Concentrate on who set out to incriminate Desmond and you'll be half way home.'

Put like that, it sounded so simple.

CHAPTER SIX

1

A CHOICE between two possible approaches presented itself and one led to Desmond. It was really a matter of clearing the decks by a process of elimination, for I considered it would be as well to dispose once and for all of the theory that he had drifted so far round the bend or become so crazed with the need to draw attention to himself as to have sent his own ridiculous letter to Scotland Yard.

The method of procedure was not immediately obvious, for although we had known each other casually for several years and had once done a provincial season together we had never had many common interests outside the theatre and I was certainly not in the habit of dropping in at his house in Notting Hill. To have invited him to lunch *à deux* would have caused the hackles of suspicion to work overtime.

However, the problem was not insoluble because there was one area of neutral territory, where my own presence would appear normal and where, with only a grain of luck, it could easily coincide with his, and this was the very same dining club where I had taken Ellen and Jeremy when she brought him along to be introduced.

Not that Desmond was much in the habit of eating there, specially during his less affluent spells, but there was a small bar on the ground floor where he was liable to drop in any morning of the week. One reason for this was that the club, which was called Le Carillon and known, inevitably, to most of its members as the Carry On, although now situated in a quiet street behind Sloane Square, had started on a more raffish note in the neighbourhood of the Charing Cross Road, at which period practically all the clientèle had been connected in some way with show business. Most had remained loyal to the club after its move up the social ladder, for the minor inconvenience was more than outweighed by its many distinctive advantages. Notable among these were the excellence and cheapness of the food, that it was a clearing house for every stray piece of theatrical gossip, that the most flamboyant and unbridled behaviour was tolerated, so long as it stopped short of setting the premises on fire; but most of all in the personality of its president, manageress and, when occasion demanded, secretary, waitress and bottle-washer. This was a formidable old dragon named Marion Lothrop, who was also a magic dragon.

No one knew much about her early history, mainly because it went back into the mists of time and Marion, although a great reminiscer by nature, was apt to be reticent about her childhood and early youth, but she had moved in theatrical circles all her adult life and had a single-minded devotion to the profession and to everyone engaged in it. She was a mine of information to those who cared to tap it, a tower of strength to anyone in trouble or distress and was loved and respected by her legion of friends, in which category, when the sun shone and hopes ran high, I ventured to include myself.

It was therefore in the full expectation of picking up some news of Desmond, if not coming face to face with him, that I dropped into Le Carillon just after midday on Friday. It was before the rush hour and there were only two other people in the bar, sitting apart from each other. One of them was a plump and ruddy man, wearing sporty tweeds, whom I vaguely recognised as an agent and who was seated in a corner near the window, reading *Variety*. There was a vast trestle table along the wall at right angles to the bar and opposite the fireplace, and it was always stacked with the latest periodicals from all over the world. It was quite an accepted thing for some members to arrive half-an-hour early for their appointments, to save themselves the expense of a subscription to *Paris-Match* or the *New Yorker*, and this man was probably one of them, for he did not bother to raise his head when I came in.

By contrast, the second member or visitor was clearly waiting for someone, for she glanced up expectantly when I opened the door, enabling me to get a good look at her in return. This was just as well, for it brought the news that she was tall and elegant in her pale suède trouser suit, had rather large hands and feet and a pile of flaxen hair rolled into a bun at the back of her head. If she happened to have come there to meet Jeremy, at least I had been forewarned.

Marion, in person, was in charge of the bar on this occasion, although taking the substantial weight off her feet by reclining in a swivel chair which had been placed beside the till. I heaved myself on to a stool and asked for a whisky sour which, after a fair amount of lumbering about, accompanied by a sing-song of muttered curses, she eventually put together.

'There you are!' she announced, plumping a large tumblerful in front of me. 'Make it last, please! I don't see myself going through all that again.'

'What's the matter?' I enquired. 'Hit by the staff shortage?'

'My little villain of a barman walked out on me the other night. Haven't found a replacement yet.'

'You mean Thomas? I should think you're better off without him. A great charmer, in my opinion, but inclined to be absent-minded.'

'So much so that when he decamped he absent-mindedly took the contents of the till and hasn't so far remembered to bring them back.'

'Oh crikey, Marion! I am sorry! Have you told the police?'

'No, and don't you dare breathe a word to your old man. His mother's a darling. She was in the wardrobe at Wyndham's for years and I'm not having her upset.'

'But Thomas might go and rob someone else, if he gets away with this one,' I said rather priggishly, having got into the way of seeing things from Robin's point of view, specially when he was not there to express it for himself.

'Can't help their troubles,' Marion said indifferently. 'They must fend for themselves, like I have to. Besides, I'm not worried about Thomas. He's got this girl friend with extravagant tastes, but he'll come crawling back in a day or two, on his knees for another chance.'

'Which you'll give him, I suppose?'

'Might do. We can't all be perfect and barmen who know their job and can speak English aren't all that thick on the ground. How did that drink turn out, by the way?'

'Lovely, thanks. I shan't have any trouble making it last.'

'Well, if you're thinking of lunching you'd better go and book a table. Madge has got a run on them today.'

'No thanks, no time for lunch. I just dropped in to say hello. Also I thought I might find Desmond here.' Having tossed out this remark, two things made me instantly aware of its having fallen like a stone on to a smooth patch of water, sending out ripples all around me. One of them was the peculiar expression which crossed Marion's face, seeming to convey a warning of some kind; the other, which I sensed rather than heard, was a kind of rustling alertness on the part of the woman sitting behind me.

Keeping perfectly still, I raised my eyebrows and goggled at Marion, who said in an offhand way:

'Well, he's here most days, but one never knows. I dare say he'll be along presently. What did you want to see him about?'

Before I could answer the door opened and two more people came in, both youngish men and both strangers to me, but evidently old friends of Marion's, for they greeted her affectionately and, on hearing the saga of Thomas, one of them removed his jacket and insisted on going through to the business side of the bar and standing in as her assistant. While all this was going on the blonde woman quietly got to her feet and slid out of the room.

'Now you've done it!' Marion said, glaring at me accusingly.

'Done what?'

'Lost the restaurant a customer, by the look of it.'

'How could I have, and who is she, anyway? I've seen her in here before, but I've never met her.'

'She's only been a member for a few weeks and I'm beginning to regret I ever let her in. Nothing but trouble and complaints. You know who introduced her?'

'No.'

'Your friend, Desmond.'

'You don't say! And you mean it was Desmond she was waiting for?'

'Shouldn't wonder. Your asking about him seems to have put the wind up her.'

'I can't see why. It was a perfectly innocuous question.'

There had been a steady influx of new arrivals while we talked, but Marion's friend had enlisted his companion's help and they had been coping fairly efficiently. However, a query had now come up concerning the whereabouts of the *crème de cassis* and Marion twisted her chair round to give the matter her full attention. Simultaneously, an arm was flung round my shoulder and a gravelly tenor voice spoke in my ear.

'Well, my little bundle of mischief, and how are we today?'

'Very well, thank you, if we means me.'

'Very well, are you?' he said, hoisting himself with infinite care on to the stool next to mine. 'Yes, you're looking well; very well indeed, one might almost say.' Even when sober, Desmond was in the habit of picking up the last speaker's words and repeating them *ad infinitum*, in this ponderous fashion. I often suspected that it was because he couldn't think of anything else to say, but it certainly slowed down the pace of conversation.

'How about you?' I enquired, to vary things a bit.

'Me?' he asked solemnly, tightening his mouth in deep thought, as though I had asked him some abstruse question, requiring intense concentration. 'Well, do you know, I'd go so far as to say I'm moderately well, all things considered.'

'What things considered?'

'What things indeed? Now there's a thought, isn't it? Shall I embark on the story of my life, or shall we regard it as an open book and proceed to order me a drink? That would appear to be the question.'

'What are you having, Desmond?' Marion said, answering it for him.

'Ah, Marion, my darling, how kind of you!' he replied, pitching his voice so that it could be heard all round the room, at the same time lifting his dark curly head to provide those on either side of him with a splendid view of his gorgeous profile. 'Would it be too much to ask for a largish scotch and soda?'

'Nothing's too much trouble for you, my boy,' she replied equably. 'Jim dear, stop playing about with that gin and tonic and give the gentleman a large scotch, please!'

'Thank you so much,' Desmond said gravely. 'Thank you very much indeed!' Then, turning back to me, he added with a ravishing smile,

'So you're well, are you?'

'Yes, we've been through all that.'

'So we have, so we have, so we have! Then what shall we talk about now? You're usually such a chatterbox. One felt one could rely on you to keep the ball of conversation spinning. Spinning, spinning, spinning,' he chanted, sweeping up his glass on the last round of circular gestures of the hand which accompanied these verbal gems.

'As a matter of fact, Desmond, there was something I wanted to ask you.'

'Ah, was there now? Something you wanted to ask me?'

'Right. From purely personal interest.'

'I was afraid of that. Purely personal interest is becoming all too common in this purely shoddy world.

However, I am prepared to indulge you. Ask away, dear child, ask away!'

'I was curious about your new friendship with Phil Roper.'

'Phil what?'

'Roper. You know, the young man at Roakes Common. Friend of Ellen's. You seem to have struck up an *entente*.'

'No, no, nothing of the kind. He rang me up, you know, that's all it was. Rung up, not struck up.'

'What for?'

The beautiful dark head went slightly out of control at this point because Desmond had flung it back at a shade too sharp an angle, in order to give emphasis to a hollow laugh, with the result that he almost tipped backwards on to the floor.

'That is something you would never, never guess,' he announced when he had recovered himself.

'I know, that's why I'm asking you. He's such a shy creature, as a rule, much too diffident, I'd have thought, to approach the celebrated Davidson. That's why I was rather intrigued to hear about it.'

'Intrigued, were you? Were you now? And how did you hear about it?'

'His mother told me.'

'Ah, his mother! How true! He has a mother, has he not? And a right old bore she is, too, I seem to remember hearing.'

'Oh, Toby doesn't like her, but that means nothing. She's okay, poor old Alison. She was a bit puzzled though by Phil going to see you,' I said, endeavouring to get back to the point.

'So was I, if you want to know. Puzzled to the depths of my lily-white soul. Time for another drink, wouldn't you say? Do me the honour of joining me, since it all goes on the slate anyway,' he said, banging his empty glass on the counter.

'No thanks, I'm making mine last. Why were you puzzled?'

'What a lot of dreary questions you ask,' he complained with an abrupt change of mood, drawing his eyebrows together in a heavy frown and fixing me with a cold and hostile look, strongly reminiscent of counsel for the defence who had got the chief prosecution witness into a tight corner. 'I am puzzled to know why you are puzzled,' he continued in a tone of quiet menace.

'I told you why.'

'Oh, did you?' he asked, picking up his newly-filled glass and promptly abandoning the courtroom scene. 'To be candid, I'd forgotten that. My memory is not always quite the thing at this hour of the morning. However, since we're being so frank with each other, I don't mind telling you that this ungainly youth telephoned to say that he had a matter of some urgency to consult me about.'

'And what was that?'

'An urgent matter that he wished to consult me about,' Desmond said, never above repeating his own last words when no others were available. 'A matter of such urgency, furthermore, that it required a private interview. You may imagine my astonishment, nay disbelief, when, having granted this oaf one hour of my valuable drinking time, I discovered that all he wanted were some professional tips.'

'On what?'

'On how to put himself across as a leaping-about, pop-singing winner of all hearts at a seaside holiday camp. Could you be more astounded?'

'Yes and no.'

'Yes and no, you say?'

'Yes.'

'I am not sure if I can accept that,' Desmond announced pompously. 'Either one is astounded, or one is not astounded. There can be no half measures in that game.'

'Yes, there can, because it was no surprise to hear he was moving into the entertainment business. I knew that already. The astonishment came from hearing he had sought your advice. Were you able to oblige?'

'No, I was not able to oblige. I felt constrained to point out that I had not served my apprenticeship on Southend pier.'

'Very proper! And what did he say to that?'

'What did who say to what? I am afraid I have forgotten what we were talking about. All I remember is that it was insufferably boring. Could we please change the subject?'

'What did Phil say when you gave him the brush?'

'Oh, still on that, are we? I don't think he said anything.'

'Nothing at all?'

'Nothing at all. Or else I wasn't listening.'

As he said this, Desmond turned his head away from me and stared straight ahead of him, blinking his eyes rather rapidly, as though the need to get Marion into focus had now become imperative. While he was working away at it, someone came up behind us and tapped him gently on the arm. It was Madge, Marion's senior lieutenant in the restaurant, a self-effacing young woman of towering efficiency and incorruptible discretion. She knew every member of the club by name, their tastes in food and wine, which tables they preferred and probably a good many more things as well, but had never been known to betray a confidence by so much as a flicker, a quality which she now proceeded to demonstrate by saying in an undertone:

'Message for you, Mr Davidson. The party you were lunching with telephoned to say they can't get here. They'll be in touch with you at the other place, later.'

'My darling Madge, how kind and thoughtful of you to tell me,' Desmond said in sonorous tones. 'I am deeply grateful, although I had quite forgotten I had a luncheon engagement and I am not feeling very hungry today, so perhaps it is all for the best. I shall treat myself to another drink instead.'

Whereupon he started banging his glass on the counter again and I polished off the dregs of the whisky sour and slid down from my stool. Not much had been gleaned from the conversation, but I knew it would be a waste of time to prolong it. Past experience informed me that Desmond had approximately one more drink to go before he passed out, and even the remote chance of picking up a nugget or two during the final lucid moments was insufficient compensation for being the one to catch him when he fell.

2

'Besides, it's my belief that I'd wrung him dry,' I told Robin. 'It's curious about Desmond, but at times he covers up remarkably well and you don't get a clue to how drunk he is until the plates start flying; he can also put on a very convincing act of being a lot further gone than he actually is.'

'He'd obviously been putting it away this morning, though,' Robin observed.

'Yes, but I noticed that as soon as Phil's name was mentioned he became much more ostentatiously drunk, yet oddly enough more articulate as well. It was as though he was really thinking about what he was saying, instead of tossing words out at random. He knew it was no use denying that Phil had approached him, but all the same I have an idea he was concealing something and thinking very hard how to handle it.'

'And what do you suppose Phil was really after, assuming this holiday camp business was just a blind?'

'Yes, I suppose he'd found that it worked with his mother, so might as well be used again; but I must say, it never sounded very convincing to me. Anyone less fitted by temperament to jolly the customers along and be the life and soul of the party would be difficult to find and I can't believe he had any real intention of applying for the job. I suppose it was the best he could think of because the poor mutt had decided that Ellen's life is in danger and he must ride forth on his white charger and protect her, or maybe protect Jeremy for her, which would be even more chivalrous. Not for nothing was he infected by her King Arthur bug.'

'And all this being brought on by his belief that Desmond was present, disguised as a waiter, when Irene picked up the wrong drink?'

'Right. Which personally I think is nonsense. Whatever Jez may say, I'm certain one of us would have recognised him. On the other hand, it would be difficult to prove because I've discovered that there was no guarantee that the other waiters would have noticed that they were one over strength, or had a stranger in their midst.'

'How did you pick that up?'

'Sheer fluke. The first time I tried to see Osgood when he was tied up with the police, I had time to waste and I used up part of it in the lounge of the Swan Hotel, and by the most fortunate coincidence I was served by one of the waiters who'd been at the reception. He's a Cypriot and he works in Soho during the winter, but every summer he transfers himself and his family to some river or coast resort where they take on extra staff for the season. It provides a nice, varied life and it's profitable, as well.'

'And I suppose something of the kind applies to most of the men employed by that catering firm?'

'Yes, with all the regattas and so forth, they have many more bookings in the summer and they take on casual staff from all over the place. There's a nucleus, of course, who are permanently employed, but the others are all quite accustomed to finding themselves working with people they've never seen before and, once he'd checked them all in, the M.C. would hardly bother to go round counting heads to make sure there wasn't one too many. All the same, I still think Phil's on the wrong track. Shall I tell you why?'

'If you would be so very kind?'

'I'll forgive the sarcasm, since you're being patient enough to listen. It's because if Desmond, in a frenzy of jealousy, had really conceived this wild scheme, it could hardly have come to him on the spur of the moment, you'll agree?'

'Yes, I suppose it's unlikely that he would have had a dose of lethal poison concealed about his person purely by chance.'

'Exactly, and if it had been planned in advance, the one thing he would have been most careful to avoid was drawing attention to himself. If he hadn't turned up in church there would have been no reason for Phil or anyone else to connect him with the murder; but he not only did turn up there, with no disguise at all, he went out of his way to ensure that everyone knew it.'

'I know, Tessa, but if you postulate that all murderers are slightly cracked in some way and Desmond, if guilty, even more so than the average, then it's no good applying logical arguments of that kind. Unless, of course, it was a deliberate trick to get attention focused on himself, so as to leave a clear field for his accomplice. In which case, it will doubtless turn out that he does have an unbreakable alibi.'

'What accomplice? You're not suggesting that Imogen was also present, disguised as a waiter and popping paraquat into the champagne?'

'Not seriously, no, but you seem to have taken a dislike to the poor woman and I thought the idea of her being involved might appeal to you. Also, you must admit, it's an odd coincidence their being so chummy.'

'Not necessarily. I see them as two star-crossed lovers getting together for a good cry and, from what Ellen tells me about her, I feel sure Imogen made all the running.'

'Nevertheless, Desmond did introduce her to his favourite haunt, making it inevitable that they would often meet, even if not by arrangement.'

'And from what I know of Desmond, he only did that to ease the way for her to pay for some of his drinks. He's always making people members and the chances are that there'll be at least one of them around every time he drops in.'

'Honestly, the more I hear about this ruffian the more I wonder that Ellen should have put up with him for so long, or why Marion does, for that matter.'

'I think she gets a bit miffed with him sometimes, but you see he's a member of the sacred profession and she believes he has great talent. In her eyes that compensates for every fault. She's right too, in a way, but he's so self-destructive that there won't be any talent left if he keeps it up. Also what you couldn't be expected to realise is that he's powerfully attractive to women and when he finds one of them attractive in return the effect can be devastating, specially in the early stages.'

'But you don't think that's how it is with him and Imogen?'

'Well, he certainly didn't seem much put out when she lost her nerve and cancelled their lunch today, if indeed it was her he was lunching with. Besides, she's not his type at all. He likes them young and nubile, everything that Ellen was, in other words. He was really demented about her and she was the one to tire first, which probably makes her even more desirable.'

'So much so as to make him resolve that if he can't have her no one else shall?'

'Oh, certainly; to the extent of writing stupid threatening letters, but nothing lasts with him and I feel sure it was just hot air. I must try and have a talk with Ellen tomorrow, incidentally. Find out if there've been any new developments over the letter. The problem will be to catch her on her own, because obviously she won't be anxious to discuss it in front of Jeremy, and as this is his so-called honeymoon there's no chance of his being out at work.'

This problem continued to nag at me at odd moments throughout the evening and I finally returned to the precept I had first thought of, which was to keep it simple. The fact was that, if Ellen were prepared to discuss the subject she was perfectly able to find the means of doing so. Nothing more was required of me than to provide the excuse and, accordingly, I resolved to telephone her in the morning and invite her to lunch. However, before I could hoist this kite into the air, the string to hold it aloft had been cut to pieces. Half-an-hour after leaving the house, Robin rang up to say that Desmond had been found dead in bed. Very few details were as yet available, but all the signs pointed to suicide or misadventure.

CHAPTER SEVEN

1

THE facts, as then known, were as follows: at eleven o'clock on the previous morning Superintendent Powell, accompanied by his sergeant and armed with the cele-brated letter, had called at No. 9 Lupton Row, where Desmond lived, which was approximately one hour before I had met him at Le Carillon. They had arrived without warning and were unable to gain admittance, since he was either out or asleep.

No. 9 was at the end of a short terrace of squat, early Victorian villas, a converted slum, which had been jazzed up with shutters and front doors of every colour of the spectrum and with window boxes and carriage lamps galore. Each house consisted of a basement kitchen and dining room, with access to the back garden, a floor just above street level and one more over that. At the time of their call the basement curtains were drawn, as were those of both the upstairs windows.

Some minutes later, returning alone and on foot, although within signalling distance of the superintendent in his car, Sergeant Blaikie, posing as a representative of the Electricity Board, had knocked at the door of No. 8.

The householder here turned out to be a young married woman, with hair all over the place and wearing a printed smock over denim trousers, who had not for an instant been taken in by this feeble ruse. Clearly, she had assumed him to be a dun and, equally clearly, was familiar with the breed and with being asked to account for her neighbour's whereabouts. In a manner at once wary and vague to the point of imbecility, she had vouchsafed that he might be away, since he quite often did go away, on tour and all that, you know, and she couldn't remember when she last saw him, but, you know, being an actor and everything, he kept odd sorts of hours and sometimes days went by, you know, without her seeing him at all.

Sergeant Blaikie did know and, wasting no more time on this unprofitable source, returned to his superior for further instructions. These were simply to remain in the car and watch for developments, reporting at regular intervals to the superintendent at his office. The sergeant intimated that he regarded this as a fairly hopeless proposition for, having encountered the young person next door, he was firmly of the opinion that her first act on closing the front door would be to pick up the telephone and warn the quarry of what was afoot. However, the superintendent reminded him that there was also the slim chance that Desmond had already gone out, leaving the curtains undrawn and would in due course return.

This indeed was the case, although it was not until five o'clock, by which time the neighbour had left her house, returned to it and shortly afterwards gone out again, this time wearing a long black skirt under the pink smock and with her hair slightly less all over the place, that the long stint was rewarded. A taxi drew up in front of No. 9 and two people got out. One of them was evidently the owner, for he used his own key, and they both went inside. Unfortunately, the sergeant could not specify the age or sex of the other person, for his view had been blocked by the taxi until the very last moment. All he could say with certainty was that he or she had been on the tall side, about the same height as Desmond, who was no shrimp, and had been wearing trousers. This, of course, proved nothing, but he inclined to the view that it had been a female because Desmond had stood aside when they entered the house, a courtesy which was accompanied by a sweeping bow.

Personally, I did not believe this to be any more conclusive than the trousers, but then Sergeant Blaikie was not familiar with the subject's antics when he had reached a certain stage of intoxication and was attempting to be humorous. Moreover, he appeared to have overlooked the fact that there were such things as platform soles.

After I had pointed this out to Robin, he went on to tell me that the sergeant had remained at his post for another ten or fifteen minutes, but there had been no further activity and the upstairs curtains had remained drawn. At which point the superintendent ordered him to call it off and return to base. It was no part of his plan to hammer on Desmond's door and then to confront him in the presence of a witness. He had been hoping to bring about a discreet and strictly private interview, and if this could not be achieved on that day it would have to wait for the next.

This, in my opinion, was where he made his biggest mistake, for when I had heard the story to the end I became convinced that, if he had forced his way into the house and had caught so much as a glimpse of that other person, Desmond would still have been alive the next time they called on him.

This, in fact, had occurred soon after nine on the following morning, somewhat earlier than planned, due to intervention on the part of Ellen. She had telephoned the local station to express her fears for Desmond's safety, having failed to get any response from his number, either between eight-thirty and midnight, or on the two further attempts she had made that morning.

Somewhat stunned by her drastic reaction to this minor contretemps, the sergeant had naturally been disposed to soothe her out of it, whereupon Ellen had positively demanded that he send someone round to the house forthwith, to ensure that all was well. However, realising that she could scarcely expect these orders to be carried out on so flimsy a pretext, she had reluctantly parted with two further items of information. One was that she knew Mr Davidson to be in a highly disturbed state of mind, having rung her up several times during the preceding few days and threatened suicide; the other that, in trying to reach him, she had used a special code which had been invented for their private convenience during the period before her marriage when they had been close friends. This was to allow the telephone to ring three times, then to replace the receiver and immediately afterwards to dial the number again. He was notorious for not answering calls when disinclined to do so, but had never been known to ignore this signal, which had been designed specifically for emergencies.

Asked to explain why Mr Davidson should not be spending the night with friends, she would only say she was certain this was not so and that the sergeant must either take her word for it, or she would have no recourse but to apply to Inspector Price of Scotland Yard, who was a close relative.

When I heard about it, I was puzzled that she had not used this lever in the first place, or better still contacted Robin direct, but concluded that the lesson he was always preaching had been too well learned and that she could only bring herself to involve him as a last resort.

In any case, whether for this or some other reason, her request was granted, at which point she rang up to warn me of what she had done, and barely an hour later the telephone rang again, bringing me first-hand news of Desmond's death. I did not stop to pass it on to Ellen, but gathered up two or three scripts which had been littering my desk for months and went out to the street to find a taxi to take me to Notting Hill. I was not immediately successful and, as the route from Beacon Square lay through all the worst conglomerations of London traffic, it was past nine-thirty when we stopped at the corner of Lupton Row and I got out.

There were three cars parked near No. 9 and a uniformed constable was stationed on the pavement outside the front door.

'Sorry, miss,' he said, stepping back a pace, as I attempted to circle round behind him, wearing an abstracted look on my face, as though unaware of his existence. 'No one allowed in there, I'm afraid.'

'Oh, really? Why not?'

'Been an accident.'

'To Mr Davidson? What happened?' I asked, looking suitably startled and apprehensive.

'Couldn't say about that. All I know is, I'm to stop here and keep everyone out.'

'Oh dear! But couldn't you just . . . ? I mean, what on earth could have happened? It must be something terribly serious for you to have been called in. Are you sure you couldn't let me inside just for one tiny second, so that I can find out?'

He shook his head in some alarm. 'More than my life would be worth. Don't you worry, they're looking after him and he'll be all right, I dare say.'

'Do you mean that, honestly?'

'Shouldn't be surprised. You're a friend of the gentleman, I take it?'

'Oh yes, a very old friend. That is, we've worked together a lot. He's an actor, you see, like me.'

'That right?'

'Yes, and you see he gave me these scripts to read, plays you know, and I was just bringing them back. He said it was most important to have them today, that's why I came so early. Oh dear, now what am I going to do?'

'If I were you, I'd hang on to them for a bit. I dare say he won't be needing them today.'

'No, I suppose not. What a pity, though! I mean, to have come all this way, specially . . . and I do hate the idea of letting him down . . .'

More stolid headshaking on his part, quickly followed by a little cheering up on mine, which led me to say: 'Oh, I know! I'll ask the girl next door. Can't remember her name, but she's awfully nice and I'm sure she'll look after them for me until Mr Davidson is better.'

'Good idea, miss, I should do that,' the constable said with immense relief as I skipped away. Not a moment too soon either, for, with my finger on the bell of No. 8, I saw him straighten up and salute, as another black car came alongside and out stepped Superintendent Powell.

2

Sergeant Blaikie's description had been reasonably accurate, but on this occasion she was wearing a man's dressing gown over the denim trousers, so obviously liked to ring the changes here and there. Her hair, on the other hand, was very much all over the place and she also looked bleary-eyed and puffy from lack of sleep. She was in the middle of a huge, engulfing yawn when she opened the door.

'Could I come in for a moment?' I asked. 'I'm a friend of Desmond's.'

'Oh yes, well, all right. What's going on over there?'

'Haven't you heard? I should have thought it might have been on the radio by now.'

'I've only just got up. We had such a night! Dick's still sleeping it off. All right for some, but I was woken by all that crashing and slamming and I thought someone must have planted a bomb or something, and we'd all have to wrap ourselves in blankets and sit in the town hall until they'd defused it or something. What happened? Has Desmond done someone in?'

'Himself, apparently.'

'You're joking!' she said, staring at me open-mouthed, and then flopped down on to a hall chest as though the muscles of her legs had collapsed.

'It's true, is it? God, how awful! People shouldn't tell you that kind of thing at this hour of the morning when you feel like I do. What happened?'

'I don't know the details. Only that he was found dead a couple of hours ago. And I'm sorry to break it so crudely, but I have a feeling the police will be knocking on your door before long and I thought you would like to be prepared.'

'What would they come here for?'

'Oh, to ask whether you'd seen anyone entering or leaving No. 9, that kind of thing.'

'Oh God, isn't it awful? I felt ghastly enough before, but this is the end! Look, we'd better go and sit down while I try and take it in,' she said, pulling herself up and traipsing off to a room at the back of the house, overlooking the miniature garden. It was furnished as a workroom and study, with pen and ink designs pinned to drawing boards on all the walls. There were two decrepit-looking armchairs, one of which had a Siamese cat on it and the other a pile of technical journals.

'My husband's an architect,' she explained, dumping the papers on to an already overloaded desk and the cat on to her lap. 'At least, he will be, if he keeps it up for another three or four years. Do you honestly not know how it happened?'

'I honestly don't, but you sound as though you considered that more important than why it happened.'

She looked up, as though seeing me in the round for the first time, and said wonderingly:

'You could be right. It rocked me when you told me, but perhaps it wasn't all that much of a surprise. He's been more than peculiar lately, ever since his girl walked out on him. No, it's not so hard to believe, only it's a shock when it happens, isn't it?'

'Well, his state of mind is one of the things the police will want to know. Another might be when you last spoke to him and whether you saw anyone going into the house or leaving it during the past twelve hours or so.'

'Why should they want to know that?'

'Because there might be someone who'd seen him more recently than you had, who could give them an up-to-date bulletin about his mood and so on.'

'You're joking! Why should anyone question what sort of mood he was in when he's just killed himself? I mean, that tells you, doesn't it?'

This was a tricky one and I could have kicked myself for not having credited her with being sufficiently wide-awake to recognise this flaw in the argument. Fortunately, she did not press the point, but went on,

'Anyway, this lovely old cat is the only one who could tell you anything. I went out early yesterday evening because I was meeting Dick at this place in Golden Square where he's training to be an architect. Then we saw some rotten film and had dinner at a Chinese place. After that we had the grisly idea of going to this party a friend of ours was giving in Islington. No use asking me what time we got home, or even how we got home. I don't remember anything special about No. 9, but I probably wouldn't have noticed if it had been burnt to the ground. And, judging by the sight of him this morning, Dick was in even worse shape than me.'

The memory of this started her yawning again and I said,

'Well, in that case, you've nothing to worry about, because once they know that they'll stop bothering you. Perhaps they won't come at all and Dick will be able to sleep in peace. I thought you'd like some advance warning, just in case.'

'Thanks,' she said, getting up and draping the sleeping cat over her shoulder. 'Nice of you to think of it.'

Before following her out of the room I tossed my scripts on to the mêlée on the desk, where I considered there was a good chance of their remaining unnoticed until after my visit was forgotten. They had served their purpose and I could at least save myself the trouble of lugging them home again. It was a small consolation and, up till then, the only one, for there was no denying that in all other respects the enterprise had not paid off, a disappointment only slightly mitigated by the belief that Superintendent Powell, were he indeed to call, was unlikely to garner any more than I had. However, this turned out to be an unnecessarily gloomy verdict, for out in the hall once more and still clasping the cat, she rubbed her face against its fur and mumbled,

'Of course, if one wanted to make a big thing out of it, like, you know, he was murdered or something, that'd be different, I suppose.'

'Oh, would it?' I asked. 'Why's that? Would you then remember that you hadn't been to a party, after all, but had been sitting here watching television and when you put the cat out you saw a furtive, bloodstained individual running down the street?'

She giggled, indulging in some more face massage, and said in a soupy voice,

'Loved one doesn't have to be put out, does he? He has his own little kitty cat door into the garden, don't you, my angel? No, but if it was something like that, you know, I mean, they wouldn't only ask us about yesterday, would they? What I mean is, they'd want to know all sorts of other things, like did he have any enemies and all that, you know, wouldn't they?'

'And did he?' I asked, crossing my fingers and clasping my hands behind my back.

'You bet! One in particular, I might add.'

'Who was that?' I asked, trying to speak without breathing.

'Well, obvious, isn't it? The one his girl chucked him over for. *Crime passionel* and all that stuff.'

'What makes you think there was bad feeling between him and Desmond?'

'Oh, come on! Well, they certainly weren't blood brothers, that's for sure,' she said, still nuzzling the cat. 'In fact, they had a great big row only the other day. I was bringing a lot of stuff back from the supermarket and I saw this feller come flying out of next door as though he'd got the Chinese army behind him. Then I heard Desmond shout something too disgusting to repeat and he slammed the door so hard I thought the whole rotten terrace would come down. The other one didn't turn round, he just galloped off into the blue.'

'I don't think that's the kind of evidence to make much impression,' I said, simulating great indifference. 'Desmond frequently lost his temper with people over complete trifles and he usually forgot about it ten minutes later. Anyway, what makes you think this other man was the one his girl left him for?'

'Because I'd seen them together, only a few weeks before. It was when Desmond gave us tickets for that play he was in at the Comedy. She and this other man were sitting a few rows in front of us. She had her hair up, which made her look different, but I recognised her because of seeing her so often going into No. 9. And they were giggling and smiling at each other the whole time, you know, so I wasn't a bit surprised when I heard that she and Desmond had split up and she was going to marry someone else.'

'And you recognised the man when you saw him here the other day? You're sure he was the same one?'

'Well, I suppose I wouldn't swear to it, cross my heart and all that . . . but sure enough.'

'All the same,' I said, choosing my words with care, 'I'd advise you to think it over a bit before you say anything. You might be asked to sign a statement, or give evidence at the inquest and it could lead to trouble unless you're a hundred per cent certain.'

The cat now displayed signs of restlessness and she removed it from her shoulder and placed it gently on the floor, whereupon it stuck its head and tail straight up in the air and stalked away in haughty disgust. The severing of this physical bond appeared to create a corresponding break in her mood, for she brushed the hairs off her smock, saying carelessly,

'Anyway, it doesn't make sense, does it? I mean, you know, it would have to be the other way round.'

'What would have to be the other way round?'

'Well, what I mean is, if this other man had pinched Desmond's girl, he wouldn't have to go and murder him as well, would he? I mean, if anyone had a grudge, it would be poor old Desmond.'

'Quite right,' I agreed, breathing normally again. 'So, on the whole, best to say nothing about it?'

'Shouldn't dream of it,' she answered with another yawn, and I believed her.

There was a florist's shop on the other side of the road and as I walked past it I had the greatest difficulty in restraining myself from going inside and asking them to send her two dozen of their finest roses.

CHAPTER EIGHT

1

'SO LOVELY old Powell is pleased, at any rate, and so, I suspect, are a few other people,' Robin concluded, when he had filled in the remaining details of Desmond's death, of which the essence was as follows:

Following the track laid down on the previous day, an officer from the Notting Hill branch had called at the house and, having failed to gain admittance, had applied next door for information. At this juncture the pattern had altered, for his repeated knocks on the door of No. 8 had met with an equally blank response. All the curtains of both houses, including those in the basement, were drawn and no clue was forthcoming as to whether any life existed behind them. Having reported this, the constable was then joined by a colleague of senior rank, equipped with the wherewithal to enter the house by force.

Entry, as the saying goes, had been effected by way of the french window from the garden, which brought them into the dining room. There was nothing to detain them there, since it did not appear to have been used for days and there was a layer of dust on the dining table. Across the passage, however, the kitchen told a different tale. There were stacks of unwashed crockery piled up in the sink, remains of stale, burnt milk and other horrors on the stove and an empty whisky bottle among the debris on the table, as well as several of its brothers in various corners and cupboards. However, there were also half-a-dozen washed glasses standing upside down on the draining board, indicating that Desmond had not been quite lost to all the niceties, and the two rooms on the ground floor were relatively clean and tidy.

The upper floor was the last to be investigated and there they had discovered the master of the house dead in his own bed. He was fully clothed except for his jacket and shoes and there was another empty whisky bottle on the chest of drawers, plus one more, a quarter full this time, on the bedside table. Also on the bedside table were one dirty glass and one empty bottle of sleeping pills and it was later established that a massive dose of the latter had been the immediate cause of death.

He had left no letter and the telephone was on its hook, which is apparently uncommon in such cases. Fingerprint experts had gone over the house, but the only prints clear enough to be of any use were found to be those of either Desmond or his daily help, who had handed in her notice a few days before, being unable to stand working in such a pigsty any longer, not to mention the language.

'So what pleases Powell about all that?' I asked.

'Well, perhaps that was making him out to be more callous than he is,' Robin conceded, 'but even if you can't go so far at this stage as to equate it with an admission of guilt, you can see how satisfactory it is in other ways? A perfectly plain case of suicide, quite in character with the victim's temperament and reputation, no complications or frills anywhere, so that wraps that one up. Conceivably, it may turn out to have no bearing whatever on Irene's death, but even so it has removed part of the undergrowth, and I might add that there are now some grounds for believing that Irene could also have taken her own life.'

'She chose an odd time for it! What prompted that pretty idea?'

'Several factors and one being that, as you know, she wasn't Mrs Osgood Lewis at all, hadn't been for years and her financial affairs had gone down a lot in recent months. She seems to have had remarkably few friends and she must have been lonely. The theory is that coming here for Ellen's wedding, at some expense to herself, could have been a last throw, gambling on the chance of being able to rebuild her life here. She might even have believed it possible that, with Ellen married and Toby on his own too, they could pick up the pieces and make a fresh start. When she saw how hopeless that was, and perhaps unable to face the prospect of returning to her dreary life in Canada, she threw in the sponge.'

'It's hard to imagine that even Irene could be so self-deluding as to entertain such hopes where Toby was concerned. She was married to him for five years and she must have known better.'

'Well, age could have mellowed him, you know. Unlike the rest of us, she was in no position to know that it had done the reverse.'

'In any case, Osgood won't have anything to do with the suicide theory and he's another who ought to know. He was far more *au courant* with the situation than any of us.'

'Oh, I dare say, but he may have axes to grind which we know nothing of.'

'I don't know why you've got such a down on Osgood, Robin. No one could have been more frank and sympathetic and he was under no sort of obligation to tell me anything. However, if it's any comfort to you, I don't rely solely on Osgood's opinion. I'm pretty sure that Irene was deliberately murdered and I happen to believe that Desmond was too.'

'Fancy that! And do you also know who by and why and all those various other little details it is so useful to possess?'

'Naturally.'

'Oh dear!' he said sadly. 'That's bad. Powell will not be pleased. Still, you may not be able to provide any proof, there's always that.'

I shook my head. 'No, there isn't. I wouldn't claim I could prove anything at this minute, but I regard myself as on the brink.'

Robin fidgeted about the room for a bit, and then he said,

'You wouldn't care to tell me what it is you've hit on and what you're proposing to do about it?'

'Quite right, I wouldn't.'

'In God's name, Tessa, why not?'

'Because I know you, my darling, and you could not love me, dear, so much, loved you not law and order more. If I were to tell you what I know, sooner or later you'd take it into your head that it was your duty to pass it on to Powell and that could be disastrous. This is a real tricky one and hearts are going to be broken and lives laid in ruins when it all comes out. Things are bad enough already without that ham-fisted, flat-footed old porcupine sticking his oar in.'

'Who gives a damn about Powell? It's you I'm thinking of.'

'Okay, so it amounts to the same thing, doesn't it? You start worrying about me and whether I'm going to get myself in some kind of fix and the next thing we know is that you're thinking the best way to protect me is to bring Powell into the act and I'm not having it. I've told you, there are more things at stake here than simply catching a criminal.'

'And you absolutely refuse to tell me what they are?'

'For the moment, yes. As I said, I can't prove anything at this stage and anyway you might not believe I was on the right track, if I were to tell you. It all hinges on so many small things. I think they add up to the right answer, but there are a few more questions to be asked before I can be sure. However, I promise you that asking them won't bring me into physical contact with the murderer. I shall be working on the fringes and my suspect won't even guess what I'm up to. There, does that satisfy you?'

'Not remotely, but I suppose I know when I'm beaten. All I ask is . . .'

'That I mind how I go and try to stay out of trouble?'

'Why do I bother?' he asked.

2

As I had stated, there were one or two questions still to be asked before I could tie up the remaining loose ends and, on the principle of starting with the simplest and working up to the climax by degrees, I telephoned Ellen and requested her to cast her mind back. She was quite equal to the task and had no difficulty or inhibitions in recalling the occasion I referred to.

'Yes, I remember it well,' she said. 'It was just after I got engaged. It was his birthday, as a matter of fact.' We then went on to speak about Desmond, saying how sad and dreadful it all was, but I was relieved to hear her discussing it in dispassionate terms, with no transports of grief. Doubtless, it was some consolation to her that she had fought to the bitter end to protect him and there was also the incontrovertible fact that, as with Powell, one major complication had now been removed. Towards the end of our conversation she admitted, in only marginally shamefaced tones, that she and Jeremy were now going ahead with their honeymoon plans.

'Oh, really? When do you leave?'

'Day after tomorrow. We're not taking the ferry, though. We've missed out on all the earlier bookings, so Jeremy thought the sensible thing would be to fly direct to Nice. We can hire a car when we get there.'

'Yes, I see. What time is your plane?'

'Four o'clock flight, so that we can have lunch at Roakes first and say goodbye. And listen, Tess, we'd like you to be there too. Think you can manage it?'

'Don't see why not. Do you want me to drive you to the airport?'

'No, thanks. That's all organised. Simon's coming too, so he can drop us off at Heathrow afterwards and take the car back to London.'

We then exchanged our *à tout a l'heures* and *à bientots* and I rang off, feeling tolerably certain that my original question had sunk like a stone in this sea of forward looking activity and would be most unlikely to surface again.

Jez came next on my list. I had two queries for her and she was inclined to be scathing about the first one.

'You could hardly expect me to give you that kind of analysis without a lot more data,' she informed me, in the stuffy voice of a surgeon who had been requested to perform an operation by telephone. So I explained that I was only interested in general trends and potentials and she grudgingly came up with some information which, while in no way confirming my theory, did nothing whatever to undermine it.

However, all this was by way of being the frill round the cutlet and when we got down to the bones of the matter she became much more decisive and was able to give me a clear and detailed account of her movements on the morning of the wedding.

I thanked her and rang off and then applied myself to working out ways and means to carry out the next item on my agenda, which, diplomatically speaking, was easily the trickiest of the lot.

CHAPTER NINE

'GOT your sheets back?' I asked, stopping to pass the time of day with Alison, who was toiling up and down the strip of grass between her hedge and the lane, bent double over the hot hand-mower.

'What?' she asked, straightening up. 'Oh yes, I did, as it happens. They came back last week, which just shows that it pays to raise the roof occasionally. Not a word of apology, mind you, but one can't expect miracles in this day and age. And what are you doing in these parts again? You seem to be very fond of us all of a sudden.'

'Lunching at Toby's. It's a sort of family reunion. Besides, I like it here.'

'Well, you needn't bother to look me up next time you come, because I shan't be here. I'm going up to Stoke-on-Trent tomorrow, to stay at my daughter's.'

'Oh, really? How long for?'

'Two or three weeks.'

'Well, that'll be nice.'

'Think so? Bleeding hard work, if you ask me,' Alison retorted, wiping the sweat from her brow with an oily hand. 'She's having another baby, did I tell you? Due at the end of the month. So old Mum's been roped in to cope while she's in hospital.'

'Oh well, makes a change, as they say. Is Phil going with you?'

'No, he's off on holiday tomorrow.'

'On his own?'

'Yes, hitch-hiking on the Continent. But he'll be staying in youth hostels, so he'll probably get in with a young crowd before long. Strikes me as a good idea, on the whole, since he can't seem to settle to anything here. That holiday camp idea fizzled out.'

'So he won't be taking the car?'

'Couldn't afford to, my dear. We haven't all been blessed with the Roxburgh millions. He's going to lend it to me while he's away. Dear old Phil, he wouldn't admit it to save his life, but I think that's what triggered off the idea of this trip. The Mini will be a godsend up there in Staffordshire, with my son-in-law out at work all day. Save me a packet in fares too. Well, I must love you and leave you, Tessa. Some of us have work to do, even if you haven't. The lunch won't cook itself and packing for both of us is no joke when you haven't a clue what the weather's going to do.'

'Pity,' I said, 'I'm too early for lunch and I was hoping to entice you up to the Bricklayers' for a quick one. Still, it's a good day for a walk on the common.'

When I had left her I drove on for another hundred yards and then took a side turning to the left, down an even narrower lane, which passed through a grove of beech trees before emerging on to open common. At this point it degenerated into a stony track, winding its way past half a dozen widely separated houses, whose front gardens fringed the common, Toby's being roughly in the centre. I could just make out Jeremy's red sports car standing by the gate.

As I had told Alison, I was in no hurry, for it was not much after midday, and a particularly halcyon one, despite her forebodings, so I parked the car on the edge of the grass and set out on foot along a path going off at right angles to the track.

Most of the surrounding flora consisted of hawthorn, brambles and gorse but at one time, before some vandal saw fit to cut it down, a magnificent sycamore must have dominated the whole area, for the stump of its trunk, which time had worn to a dark grey polish, was about ten feet in diameter. This was the spot which had been known in Ellen's childhood as King Arthur's throne and, as it was out of sight of the house, being concealed on three sides by bushes and saplings, it had made an ideal setting for all kinds of apocryphal exploits in the career of her hero. I sat down on the trunk, remembering how Ellen had sat there on her wedding morning and how she had been discovered by Jeremy, out for an early morning stroll on the common.

It so happened that I too was now about to be discovered by someone strolling on the common, although he was not the one I was expecting. Even before he approached I could see from the cloud of candy floss hair that it was Simon.

'Ah,' he said, as he saw me and came nearer. 'What a coincidence to find you here! And looking every inch the *belle dame sans merci*, if I may pass the remark.'

'Why is it a coincidence?'

'Because I had been thinking about you, do you see, and deciding that it might be a practical plan to fall in love with you. You wouldn't object to that, I trust? It would only be in a very remote way, you know. I should be content to adore you from afar.'

'Oh, very well, in that case, I have no particular objection.'

'You wouldn't be called upon to reciprocate or anything like that. Just throw me an occasional bone, or perhaps have dinner with me once in a while when your husband is busy putting the finishing touches to a sensational murder case. I am rather a Jamesian character, in some ways.'

'Yes, I guessed you might be.'

'Largely cultivated, of course, so it is all the more gratifying to find that it has not passed unobserved. To tell you the truth, I had toyed with the idea of falling in love with Ellen. It wouldn't have been at all difficult, and rather convenient in many ways, but then I thought there might be something a little incestuous about it, almost claustrophobic, if you know what I mean?'

'Yes, I do know.'

'Being remote and claustrophobic at the same time might have been rather taxing.'

'I agree.'

'There was another slight snag too,' he admitted after a brief pause.

'Oh, really?'

'I had a nasty feeling that she might not even notice that I was in love with her, and I don't think that would be entirely satisfactory, do you? I am all in favour of adoring from afar, but I think I should want it to be noticed and Ellen is so loopy about that brother of mine that I sometimes wonder if she is aware of the existence of another male.'

'You really believe that?'

'With my hand on my heart.'

'I see.'

'Well, it's nice to have had this little chat and got every-thing fixed up,' Simon said. 'We appear to be mentally attuned, which is always a good start. I dare say our relationship will blossom into something so subtle and delicate that we shall hardly need to communicate at all. Or would that be rather dull? I shall have to work on it and see if I can find an acceptable compromise. In any case you seem to be rather pensive so perhaps it would show the right sort of sensibility on my part if I were to continue my walk now and leave you to your dreams.'

'I think that might be best, only they are not dreams, they are nightmares.'

'How obtuse of me not to have realised. Well, I am forever at your side, remember. Spiritually, if nothing else.'

'Thank you,' I said, and he strolled away and was soon out of sight.

Nevertheless, it was Robin who saved the day and I was glad of that too. Bone scattering and being adored from afar are all very well in their place, but when you get right down to it it's the one who saves your skull from being battered to a pulp who really earns your love and gratitude and it is always a pleasure to bestow these on the nearest and dearest.

Nonetheless, it is only fair to concede that Simon had probably contributed his share, for undeniably his presence had forced my assailant to delay matters and to remain hidden until the coast was clear, thus enabling Robin to catch up with him, jump on him from behind, remove the spanner from his hand and knock him unconscious.

In fact, I had been alone on my tree trunk for only a couple of minutes after Simon disappeared from view and was beginning to wonder if I was wasting my time and would do better to gird my loins and face the family reunion, when I heard a sharp cry behind me and instinctively stood up and faced the other way. The cry was repeated, but from the same distance, and was followed by grunts and gurgles and scuffling noises, all suggesting that the latest arrival was not alone. So I took a few cautious steps in the direction the noises were coming from. Only a few were needed because the next minute Robin came bursting through into Arthur's throne room, with twigs in his hair and carrying a spanner, which he waved at me in a marked manner.

'You thumped him, did you?' I asked.

'Yes. Get up to the house as quick as you can and telephone, will you? I must get back and keep an eye on him. He's out cold at the moment, but we don't want him coming to and starting any more mayhem.'

He disappeared into the bushes again and I sprinted out on to the common. It might have been quicker to take the car, but one's instinct in these crises is to trust to one's own legs rather than internal combustion and there was a short cut by a footpath which took me diagonally across the common. It led to the manor house, over on my left and used now as offices for a firm of farm machinery manufacturers. They had three or four telephone lines and I knew that I should be allowed to conduct my business in the privacy which would be so signally lacking in Toby's hall.

When it was concluded I remained motionless, staring out of the window of the tiny office that had been allocated to me, not seeing anything, but urging myself on to perform the most disagreeable and difficult task I had ever been faced with. Finally, I took a couple of deep breaths and when I had let out the second one I rang up Alison.

CHAPTER TEN

'So TELL me how you guessed,' I said.

Two hours had passed and Robin and I were in the summer house, Toby having exerted himself to go indoors and sound out the chances of Mrs Parkes bringing us some tea, when she could tear herself away from the various friends and relatives who had just happened to be passing, or had run over to borrow a crochet pattern. They had been painful and distressing hours and at the end of them the young couple had been prevailed upon only with difficulty to be driven to the airport and to embark at last on their honeymoon. Ellen had been in tears again at the moment of departure, but at least there could be no doubt as to whose broad shoulder she was weeping on, as Simon was quick to point out, with a heavy wink and most un-Jamesian jerk of the thumb.

'I take no credit for it,' Robin replied. 'It was Jez who put me on your track.'

'How did she get into it?'

'I can't quite understand it myself, but perhaps she really does possess second sight, or at any rate a more highly developed first one than the rest of us. She rang up and told me about a strange feeling she had that you were heading for some kind of trouble. I remember her mentioning the vibrations being wrong and the yang dominating the yin in some way, which apparently bodes no good in her philosophy.'

'And you took that seriously and acted on it? You stagger me!'

'Well, only because this yang business was partially founded on some factual evidence which was within my comprehension. Apparently she had been alerted by an undercurrent of excitement in your voice.'

'I don't call that very factual.'

'Moreover,' Robin continued, as though I had not spoken, 'you asked her for a character analysis about people with birthdays between the last week of April and the first week of May.'

'Yes, that's true.'

'That surprised her very much. In the past, your attitude to the subject has been somewhat sceptical. She had scarcely expected to find a convert in you.'

'I was not out to be converted. It was simply a device to get her talking. It is always good strategy to begin in that way. By the time you get to the nub the reserves are down and you actually get a spontaneous answer. Of course, if she had told me that people born under that sign are invariably mild, sweet-tempered and incapable of violence, it might have set me back a bit. I couldn't swear to that, but in fact she told me nothing of the kind, so it hardly mattered, one way or the other.'

'It might have occurred to you, though, that all Ellen's friends had been well and truly put under the horoscope.

It was Jez's first thought when Jeremy was taken to the flat to be introduced, and she is very business-like in her work, you know. She operates on a card index system, so it was a simple matter to check through the records and identify the person you had in mind.'

'Nevertheless, she could hardly deduce anything sinister from that. I said nothing about his being a murderer.'

'No, but you did go on to ask her about her movements on the wedding day, with specific reference to Ellen's address book. Furthermore it transpired that you were not interested in its career before it left London, only in what became of it when it reached this house. Jez is no fool, I might tell you, and it didn't take her any longer than it did us to realise that whoever had removed Desmond's letter and sent it to the police was very likely Irene's murderer. The fact that you evidently believed that it had been stolen after it arrived here, combined with your interest in Phil's horoscope, rather narrowed the field, which was why she became apprehensive. I knew you were spending the day here so I thought it might be a bright idea to join the party.'

'Well, I suppose I should be grateful to her and I am, but I wouldn't have been taken off guard, you know. I was expecting Phil to follow me on to the common. I was even prepared for him to get rough, but he always crumbled when faced by a bossy female and I didn't anticipate any serious trouble.'

'What made you so sure he would come after you?'

'Oh, it was Alison telling me she had to cook the lunch. I know she never bothers when she's alone. Therefore, Phil was at home and therefore he would have seen me talking to his mother. I was certain he would put her through a stiff cross-examination about everything I'd said.'

'And what, may one ask, did you say which so put the wind up him, that he followed you on to the common, armed with a spanner?'

'Well,' I replied thoughtfully. 'It may have been principally my question about the sheets.'

'Sheets?' Robin repeated incredulously. 'What sheets?'

'The pair that had been mislaid by the laundry. The very first time that Alison mentioned them something clicked and from that moment Phil began to figure as a suspect. Immediately afterwards I had another stroke of luck because when I had my talk with Osgood he presented me with a motive at last. That meant that Irene had been the intended victim all along and I began to see things more clearly. After that, everything fell into place and it was simply a question of finding the proof.'

'Which came to you by courtesy of a pair of missing sheets?'

'They were part of it. It occurred to me at the time that there was something odd there. To lose one sheet is a thing that might happen to any laundry, but a pair of them, with no explanation at all, not even an apology, was surely stretching it, specially as they have a virtual monopoly in these parts and Alison must have been a regular customer ever since she's lived here. Anyway, it set me thinking and eventually I traced the connection.'

'I am delighted to hear that,' Robin said in a heart felt voice. 'And I hope to trace it myself in due course, though it does elude me at present.'

'That's only because you didn't arrive here until just before the wedding,' I told him. 'And by then, although none of us had any idea of it, the story was already half way through. You see, those sheets belong to the period when Phil was going all out to set Jeremy up as the scapegoat. Actually, that plan didn't work very well and later, when he got his hands on the letter, he dropped Jeremy and switched to Desmond, but on the day before the wedding Jeremy was his man and he did everything he could to incriminate him. It must have seemed like the perfect answer too because, if it had succeeded, Phil would not only have got away with his own crime but Ellen would have been free to be comforted and wooed and perhaps this time won. So when he woke up on the wedding day and found that Jeremy had already gone out and that his car had gone too, he decided to make capital out of it. He whipped the sheets off Jeremy's bed, replaced them with a clean pair and told his mother that the naughty bridegroom had been out all night. The used sheets had been bundled away somewhere and were probably later taken to the launderette, before being returned to the linen cupboard. At least, I imagine that's how it was, although it will be old Powell's job to tie up all the routine stuff.'

'I still don't get the point, you know,' Robin complained. 'I mean, granted that it was very reprehensible of him, was there really anything incriminating in Jeremy's having spent the night elsewhere?'

'Not in itself, no, but it was all part of the build-up to discredit him; what the politicians call a smear campaign. You see, if it had come to the crunch and questions had been asked, it would have been Phil's word against Jeremy's, with those unused sheets to show which one was speaking the truth, for why should Phil lie over a thing like that? I can tell you why: so as to create a climate in which Jeremy is seen to be not only a liar, but incapable of giving any account of how he spent the whole of one night, and the night before his wedding at that. How easy would be the next step; to believe that he was also a hit-and-run driver, who could dine with his family and appear perfectly at ease, having just left a child to die by the roadside.'

'Ah!'

'Though, mind you, that wasn't the only thing Phil did to blacken his character. In fact, if anyone was away from his bed for most of that night it was he. It must have taken him quite a while, working quietly away in his own garage, with the doors shut, duplicating the dents and damage to his own car on to Jeremy's. Though he must have botched it, poor stupid Phil, because the police undoubtedly made enquiries at local garages about any emergency repairs they'd carried out and if Fairman's had come up with anything suspicious about Jeremy's little job we'd certainly have heard about it.'

'And when did Phil manage to tidy up the Mini?'

'Earlier in the evening, I should imagine, when the others came over here to meet the Roxburghs, Phil having made the excuse that he had to work. Alison secretly believed he had stayed away because he couldn't bear to be in the same room with Ellen and her new love, and I dare say that he was quite pleased to foster that illusion, but it's more likely that he needed the time to straighten out his own bumper and headlamp.'

'Even that was leaving it rather late, though. Surely there was a risk of someone having noticed the damage already?'

'Not if he'd put it straight into the garage when he brought Irene home. She was presumed to be in far too hysterical a state to have noticed a thing like that and when Owen flagged him down on the hill, he was careful to drive on for quite a distance before stopping, to ensure that Owen would only get a very dim, rear view of the Mini. Besides, who in the world would have noticed a few extra bumps and scratches on that old rattletrap? There were too many there already for any fresh ones to stand out and Phil was forever patching it up, bit by bit. In fact, I should guess that it was being such an old crock that drew Irene's attention to it in the first place. By which I mean that, when it came down the hill and Owen hailed it, she remembered that only a few minutes earlier she had watched it travelling up the hill.'

'So you think that's what happened?'

'Don't you? You'll remember that Irene was sitting in Owen's taxi, ostensibly having a nervous breakdown, but, knowing her, more likely inspired by the determination to avoid unpleasantness, and I dare say she wasn't missing much. Her ex-husband told me that she was very observant and just loved nosing out nasty little home truths, and when Phil said nothing whatever, either then or later, about having driven up the hill just before he came down it, she probably realised she was on to something and eventually to guess that when he came down he was doing so for the second time. She may even have teased him with hints to that effect and she certainly made it plain to everyone she met that she had some interesting information for the police.'

'So your theory is that, having run over the boy on the first time down, he continued on to the bottom and then presumably turned into a lane and removed any stains or fragments of clothing from his car. But why on earth should he have then gone back up again, to revisit the scene of the crime, so to speak?'

'Well, he must have had a frightful shock and presumably he wasn't then the hardened criminal he later became, so it would have been a natural impulse. Probably he was praying like mad that he'd find the boy sitting by the road with nothing more serious than a bruised knee, or at the very least that some other motorist was taking care of him, which in fact was exactly what he did find.'

'All right, I can accept that, but, having reached the top once more, why come down the hill yet again? Surely the impulse by then would have been to turn tail and take another route home?'

'Oh, I have the answer to that one too.'

'Have you really?' Robin asked without much enthusiasm.

'You see, in that brief glimpse, the only face he could see at all clearly was Irene's, a complete stranger to him. He could have no idea that the man with his back to him bending over the boy, was Owen and that the next time he went past he'd be compelled to stop, or get himself into even deeper trouble. Also he'd really left himself no choice about which route to take. He had to cross the river somewhere and if he didn't do so at Stadhampton it would have taken him miles out of his way. He'd already caused himself quite a lot of delay and there was still his mother's weekend shopping to do. If he didn't get to Stadhampton before everything closed down, he'd have had one hell of a job accounting for how he'd spent the time.'

There was a rattle of china and Toby entered, down centre, carrying the tea tray.

'Mrs Parkes is beside herself with excitement,' he explained. 'There is simply no holding her and nothing for it but to see to all this myself. However, I hope I'm in time for the *dénouement*. Tessa is inclined to spare us no detail when she is describing her own triumphs, but I am bound to say that the *dénouement* is the only part which really grips me.'

'There is no *dénouement* to speak of,' I said stiffly, 'beyond what Robin achieved when he knocked Phil cold on the common; and very few triumphs either. I had all the breaks and all the best opportunities to see what was afoot.'

'Perhaps you can still scrape up a few surprises for us, though?' Robin suggested in a consoling voice. 'Such as how Phil got the poison to Irene and how and why he killed Desmond.'

'The first one is easy,' I replied. 'Alison is a dedicated gardener, but obviously she couldn't afford expensive weed killers. Phil had studied agriculture at the university and must have been in the way of procuring paraquat for her, in concentrated form, which, when the moment came, he fed to Irene.'

'But when was that moment?'

'Any old time; in her early tea, her breakfast coffee, her scotch and soda, but probably more than once. I looked it up and, although it's a poison which is fatal in large enough doses, it doesn't take immediate effect. In fact, there's more likely to be a delay of several hours.'

Toby glanced enquiringly at Robin, who nodded back and said,

'Yes, there's always been evidence to suggest there was no poison either in her last drink or in the pills, although Powell chose to keep that under his hat. It widened the field, you see, because the murderer didn't have to be present when death actually occurred.'

'And I feel sure Phil devoutly hoped not to be,' I went on. 'Alison badgered him into taking her to the wedding, but when she sent him home to fetch her shoes he flew off like a bird on the wing and I don't suppose he had any real intention of returning. However, when in my somnolence I allowed the telephone to go on ringing and ringing he must have felt that the furies were after him; or maybe the habit of obedience to his mother proved too strong. Anyway, back he came and by that time he'd read Desmond's letter and substituted him for the scapegoat. All those wild threats must have seemed like the answer to a prayer.'

'So that was when he got hold of the letter, was it?' Toby asked. 'I always winder that anyone should read other people's correspondence! I have enough trouble with my own.'

'I suppose Phil saw the address book, with everything tumbling out of it, when he passed the front door. Some of Caspar's work there, no doubt, for I don't think even Jez would have been so careless. Phil was in no hurry and he probably stopped to pick it up, as one would, but never got further than Desmond's letter, which presumably went straight into his pocket after a single glance at the contents, and the first thing he did, when I met him coming back with the shoes, was to float the idea that one of the waiters was actually Desmond in disguise which one wasn't totally unprepared to accept after that ridiculous scene in the church. Unfortunately, as with so many of Phil's clever schemes, this one hardly got off the ground, so he decided to tickle things up by sending the letter to Scotland Yard.'

'And now you really have scraped up a surprise for us,' Toby said admiringly. 'For what astonishes me is that he should then have killed Desmond. In the circumstances, one would rather have expected it to be the other way round.'

'Ah, but you see, if this campaign was to succeed, it was essential to find out whether Desmond had a solid alibi for the period after he was thrown out of church, and I think Phil was plugging away at that for quite a while.'

'Until he found to his chagrin that Desmond did have an alibi, so was obliged to kill him and make it look like suicide?'

'Either that, or Desmond saw through him and hit on the truth. He wasn't entirely composed of hot air and alcohol, you know, and, like many actors, he was extremely observant,' I said, modestly lowering my eyes.

As this brought no response from the audience, I went on,

'He was also completely amoral and, although he might have twitted Phil with it, he wouldn't have dreamt of turning him in; but of course there was no knowing what he might say in his cups and I dare say Phil realised that his only permanent safety lay in grabbing the opportunity to get Desmond totally stoned and then to tip a few dozen sleeping pills into his nightcap. There can't have been much problem about it because, as I learnt from the girl next door, he had already been in the house at least once before. As a matter of fact, she mistook him for Ellen's new love, but that was because she'd seen them at the theatre together. Somehow, I didn't think Ellen would have practised putting her hair up when she was out with Jeremy, for it was meant to be a surprise. And, anyway, Jeremy's a Scorpio,' I added by way of postscript, 'so his birthday must be in the autumn.'

'What's that got to do with anything?' Robin asked, being the one to show surprise now.

'Nothing whatever. I just threw it in as an example of how lucky I was in being so close to the heart of things and in knowing so much about all the case histories. With the exception of Jeremy, who was a bit of an enigma to start with, I had the advantage of knowing all the protagonists so much more intimately than either of you did. Even Ellen, I think you would admit, Toby, is in some ways a closed book to you?'

'I prefer it so,' Toby replied. 'I love her dearly and to me her looks and character leave nothing to be desired. If I knew her as you do, as a contemporary, that is, I might find sides to her that were less than perfect, and that would not suit me at all. I think that probably sums up what I have heard described as the generation gap,' he added, solemnly raising his tea cup. 'If so, let us drink to its continuance!'

THE END

FELICITY SHAW

THE detective novels of Anne Morice seem rather to reflect the actual life and background of the author, whose full married name was Felicity Anne Morice Worthington Shaw. Felicity was born in the county of Kent on February 18, 1916, one of four daughters of Harry Edward Worthington, a well-loved village doctor, and his pretty young wife, Muriel Rose Morice. Seemingly this is an unexceptional provenance for an English mystery writer—yet in fact Felicity's complicated ancestry was like something out of a classic English mystery, with several cases of children born on the wrong side of the blanket to prominent sires and their humbly born paramours. Her mother Muriel Rose was the natural daughter of dressmaker Rebecca Garnett Gould and Charles John Morice, a Harrow graduate and footballer who played in the 1872 England/Scotland match. Doffing his football kit after this triumph, Charles became a stockbroker like his father, his brothers and his nephew Percy John de Paravicini, son of Baron James Prior de Paravicini and Charles' only surviving sister, Valentina Antoinette Sampayo Morice. (Of Scottish mercantile origin, the Morices had extensive Portuguese business connections.) Charles also found time, when not playing the fields of sport or commerce, to father a pair of out-of-wedlock children with a coachman's daughter, Clementina Frances Turvey, whom he would later marry.

Her mother having passed away when she was only four years old, Muriel Rose was raised by her half-sister Kitty, who had wed a commercial traveler, at the village of Birchington-on-Sea, Kent, near the city of Margate.

There she met kindly local doctor Harry Worthington when he treated her during a local measles outbreak. The case of measles led to marriage between the physician and his patient, with the couple wedding in 1904, when Harry was thirty-six and Muriel Rose but twenty-two. Together Harry and Muriel Rose had a daughter, Elizabeth, in 1906. However Muriel Rose's three later daughters—Angela, Felicity and Yvonne—were fathered by another man, London playwright Frederick Leonard Lonsdale, the author of such popular stage works (many of them adapted as films) as *On Approval* and *The Last of Mrs. Cheyney* as well as being the most steady of Muriel Rose's many lovers.

Unfortunately for Muriel Rose, Lonsdale's interest in her evaporated as his stage success mounted. The playwright proposed pensioning off his discarded mistress with an annual stipend of one hundred pounds apiece for each of his natural daughters, provided that he and Muriel Rose never met again. The offer was accepted, although Muriel Rose, a woman of golden flights and fancies who romantically went by the name Lucy Glitters (she told her daughters that her father had christened her with this appellation on account of his having won a bet on a horse by that name on the day she was born), never got over the rejection. Meanwhile, "poor Dr. Worthington" as he was now known, had come down with Parkinson's Disease and he was packed off with a nurse to a cottage while "Lucy Glitters," now in straitened financial circumstances by her standards, moved with her daughters to a maisonette above a cake shop in Belgravia, London, in a bid to get the girls established. Felicity's older sister Angela went into acting for a profession, and her mother's theatrical ambition for her daughter is said to have been the inspiration for Noel Coward's amusingly imploring 1935 hit song "Don't Put Your Daughter on the Stage, Mrs. Worthington." Angela's greatest contribution to the cause of thespianism by far came when she married actor and theatrical agent Robin Fox, with whom she produced England's Fox acting dynasty, including her sons Edward and James and grandchildren Laurence, Jack, Emilia and Freddie.

Felicity meanwhile went to work in the office of the GPO Film Unit, a subdivision of the United Kingdom's General Post Office established in 1933 to produce documentary films. Her daughter Mary Premila Boseman has written that it was at the GPO Film Unit that the "pretty and fashionably slim" Felicity met documentarian Alexander Shaw—"good looking, strong featured, dark haired and with strange brown eyes between yellow and green"—and told herself "that's the man I'm going to marry," which she did. During the Thirties and Forties Alex produced and/or directed over a score of prestige documentaries, including *Tank Patrol*, *Our Country* (introduced by actor Burgess Meredith) and *Penicillin*. After World War Two Alex worked with the United Nations agencies UNESCO and UNRWA and he and Felicity and their three children resided in developing nations all around the world. Felicity's daughter Mary recalls that Felicity "set up house in most of these places adapting to each circumstance. Furniture and curtains and so on were made of local materials. . . . The only possession that followed us everywhere from England was the box of Christmas decorations, practically heirlooms, fragile and attractive and unbroken throughout.

In Wad Medani in the Sudan they hung on a thorn bush and looked charming."

It was during these years that Felicity began writing fiction, eventually publishing two fine mainstream novels, *The Happy Exiles* (1956) and *Sun-Trap* (1958). The former novel, a lightly satirical comedy of manners about British and American expatriates in an unnamed British colony during the dying days of the Empire, received particularly good reviews and was published in both the United Kingdom and the United States, but after a nasty bout with malaria and the death, back in England, of her mother Lucy Glitters, Felicity put writing aside for more than a decade, until under her pseudonym Anne Morice, drawn from her two middle names, she successfully launched her Tessa Crichton mystery series in 1970. "From the royalties of these books," notes Mary Premila Boseman, "she was able to buy a house in Hambleden, near Henley-on-Thames; this was the first of our houses that wasn't rented." Felicity spent a great deal more time in the home country during the last two decades of her life, gardening and cooking for friends (though she herself when alone subsisted on a diet of black coffee and watercress) and industriously spinning her tales of genteel English murder in locales much like that in which she now resided. Sometimes she joined Alex in his overseas travels to different places, including Washington, D.C., which she wrote about with characteristic wryness in her 1977 detective novel *Murder with Mimicry* ("a nice lively book saturated with show business," pronounced the *New York Times Book Review*). Felicity Shaw lived a full life of richly varied experiences, which are rewardingly reflected in her books, the last of which was published posthumously in 1990, a year after her death at the age of seventy-three on May 18th, 1989.

Curtis Evans